Hit and Run?

He was tall and dark-haired. His face was extremely bony. That was all Kirsten noticed before he took a step toward her approaching car.

"Watch it!" Mr. Busk bellowed.

"Oh oh oh oh oh oh!" Gwen gasped.

Kirsten and Mr. Busk jammed their feet on the brakes.

EEEEEEEEEEEEE.

Thump.

With a dull cry, the boy fell to the blacktop.

Also by Peter Lerangis:

The Yearbook

DRIVER'S DEAD

PETER LERANGIS

SCHOLASTIC INC.
New York Toronto London Auckland Sydney

No part of this publication may be reproduced in whole or in any part, or stored in a retrieval system, or transmitted in any form or by any means, electronic, mechanical, photocopying, recording, or otherwise, without written permission of the publisher. For information regarding permission, write to Scholastic Inc., 555 Broadway, New York, NY 10012.

ISBN 0-590-46677-1

12 11 10 9 8 7 6 5 4 3 2 1   4 5 6 7 8 9/9

Printed in the U.S.A.   01

First Scholastic printing, October 1994

For Nick and Joe,
always

Prologue

Nguyen

Hot.

She is hot.

He cannot stop thinking about her.

He lifts his fingers from his computer, but the rain keeps on tapping outside his window.

Time to go.

He looks up at the photo again. It's on his wall, just below the Lamborghini poster and to the right of the Ferrari shot.

She's in profile. Close up. Her smile is amazing. He wants that smile. All for himself. Now. Before he leaves.

He closes his eyes and concentrates. The rumbling sound begins.

Move.

It hasn't happened. He knows it. Sweat tickles his forehead. His teeth grind together.

Move NOW!

He is vibrating. He is going to pass out.

Dumb idea. Rob is waiting for him in the rain. He has to go.

He opens his eyes. For a moment he sees nothing. The room is red and black.

Then everything clears.

Nguyen looks at the photo again.

He grins. It has worked.

Gwen is still smiling. But she looks different. She has turned.

She is now facing him.

Virgil

"He's not coming." Virgil Garth looks up the road. A block away, a street lamp is steaming against the cold April drizzle.

No one is going to meet him and Rob on a night like this. No one in his right mind.

Least of all a guy who's been invited for a "talk" with Rob Maxson. A talk about going out with the wrong girl.

A shakedown. That's what they called this in crime novels.

This whole idea is crazy.

But Virgil isn't about to say that. Not to Rob. No way.

"He'll come." Rob leans against the car. As he hunches his shoulders, his face sinks into his black leather jacket collar. He lifts a cigarette, his hand cupped over the top, and takes a drag. His fingernails are black with axle grease.

In the street lamp's dim ash-gray light, Rob's bony face looks like a skull. Virgil wonders why girls fall all over him. Why Gwen Mitchell, of all people? She's hot. Red hair, killer smile. But Rob? Okay, the green eyes. Girls think those are cool. But that face looks as if someone had chiseled it out of slate in a hurry with a rough blade.

Maybe if Gwen could see Rob now, she'd have second thoughts.

But Gwen isn't the one due to show up. Her new quote-unquote boyfriend is. The Vietnamese guy. Nguyen.

Nguyen the Meek and Invisible. Nguyen of the plaid shirts and pocket protectors, who has been drooling after Gwen since sophomore year. Who tried to win her with . . . magic tricks. That's right, folks. Making newspapers catch fire on the other side of the room, levitating ashtrays, making objects disappear from photos.

What a way to get a girl. Very cool. Cutting-edge sexy. Zzzzzzz.

Virgil remembers Gwen talking about the tricks. She was laughing. Rolling her eyes. Hysterical.

The worst thing is, Nguyen thinks it worked. Gwen's been glomming all over him. Why? She thinks Rob will be jealous.

Dumb move. Rob couldn't care less about her.

Virgil, on the other hand, could. If Gwen had to glom, why couldn't she have picked him?

Rob blows the smoke away from Virgil, but the wind pushes it back.

Virgil coughs. He walks around the rusted Toyota and enters the passenger side. The car smells of Old Spice and wet dog.

But it's dry. It beats rain and cigarette smoke. Well, just barely.

Virgil rolls down his window an inch. "Where'd you get this junker?"

"Borrowed it."

"Whose is it?"

"Someone's."

Virgil rubs his forehead. "Someone you know?"

He hears Rob exhale, sees him shift weight from one hip to the other. No answer.

Oh, great. Accessory to a grand larceny. Aiding and abetting an unlicensed driver. Juvenile court . . . or are sixteen-year-olds tried as adults in New York State?

"Don't you think this whole thing is a little . . . you know, extreme?" Virgil says.

The keys hurtle through the window and land in his lap with a loud jangle. Virgil glances in the rearview mirror. Rob is booking.

"Hey!" Virgil scrambles out of the car. "Where are you going? I don't know how to drive!"

"Walk," Rob says without turning.

"It's, like, two miles. In the rain. Don't leave me here. This was your idea!"

Rob spins around. He flicks his cigarette and it hisses as it lands in a puddle. "You think I'm doing this for me?"

It's a good question, but Virgil doesn't answer.

"You wanted me to do you a favor, right?" Rob barges on. "So here I am, standing in the rain like a jackass. Why? Because you can't get a girl by yourself."

"I just wanted you to, you know, talk to her — "

"If I talk to her, she thinks I'm in love. I'll never get rid of her." Rob comes face to face with Virgil. "I am doing this for you. Listen, you want Gwen or not?"

"Yeah."

"You want Viet Nerd out of her life?"

Virgil winces. Terrific. Rob's a racist, too. "Look, let's just go home, okay? I mean, I don't hate Nguyen like you do, so why don't you and he — "

"Don't hate him? Look at your history, dude. We lose a war to these people — and then they come in and take our jobs. My dad's job."

"I don't want to get into this, Rob. Just tell me what you're going to do to him."

"It's like I told you — a talk. Nothing too crazy — a little drive, a little conversation — and boom, he gets the message. He stays away from Gwen . . . and you can move in. Cool?"

Before Virgil can answer, he hears the clicking of a ten-speed bike behind Rob.

Nguyen Trang rides into the pool of light under the street lamp. He stops and gets off his bike.

Go. Go now! Virgil has the urge to scream it out.

But that would really get Rob angry. Virgil isn't stupid enough to do that.

Rob sees the look in his eyes and turns around. "Heyyy, Trang, how's every little thang?"

He meets Nguyen outside the light, where it fades into darkness, and throws his arm around his shoulder. "Come for a ride with Virgil and me."

Nguyen smiles uncertainly as he looks at the Toyota. "This is the car you found in the woods? You said it was a Ferrari or something."

What an alibi. Rob knows Nguyen is a car fanatic.

"I meant a Toyota." Rob leads Nguyen to the passenger side and opens the door. "Anyway, I got it running."

Nguyen looks at him suspiciously. "Yeah? So why didn't you pick me up at my house?"

"Sorry," Rob says with a laugh. "Come on, get in."

"Where am I supposed to leave my bike?"

"Anywhere. We'll be back in a minute."

Nguyen drops his bike. Rob pushes him into the car and gestures toward Virgil to get in, too. Then he runs around to the driver's side.

In seconds Rob is peeling down the winding

road, deeper into the wooded area between Port Lincoln and Fenimore Village. The car's old windshield wipers flatten the raindrops into thick, wide curves.

"Where are you going?" Nguyen asks.

Rob grins. He yanks the steering wheel to the left. Nguyen's shoulder jams against Virgil's.

Now Virgil feels the heat of Nguyen's gaze. He turns away from the questioning eyes and puts on his seat belt.

"Turn on my headlights," Rob says.

"What?" Nguyen asks.

"You know, just by thinking about it. I hear you can do that."

Nguyen stares at him. "Who told you — "

"Tell us how you feel about Gwen," Rob interrupts.

"Is that what this is about?" Nguyen snaps. "What do you care how I feel?"

"You love her, huh?" Rob says in a mocking tone.

"What's it to you?"

"What's it to her? Not much, I think." Rob laughs. "Right, Virgil?"

Virgil freezes. But he hasn't heard the question.

A horn is blaring.

Two headlights are bearing down on them. Swerving from side to side.

Rob's eyes widen. He leans on the horn. "YO! YOU'RE IN THE WRONG LANE!"

Rob slams on the brake. The car starts to skid. He pulls the steering wheel to the left. The headlights follow them.

Virgil's knuckles whiten as he grips the dashboard. The car spins out on the wet road. When Rob gains control, a metal guardrail looms in front of them.

Beyond that, the road drops off into a steep ravine.

"STRAIGHTEN OUT!" Virgil yells.

But the blast of the other car's horn drowns him out. Along with the sound of the brakes. And the shrieking of Nguyen Trang.

With a jarring smash, the car hits the guardrail. Virgil sees a flash of red in the windshield.

Then he blacks out.

Chapter 1

KIRSTEN WILKES
PRIVATE JOURNAL!!
PENALTY FOR READING: DEATH

September 22

Three thousand dollars. That's how much the accident is going to cost. Because I hit a tree with Dad's car at, like, two miles an hour. Can you believe it? The tree had more damage than the car!

Dad was mad. He almost had a heart attack because I hit it on the passenger side, where he was sitting. But he says the insurance company will pay for it, so I shouldn't worry about the money part.

It doesn't matter. I feel like an idiot! AUUUUUUGGGGHHH!

I will never *never NEVER* learn to drive well. You know what happened in driver's ed Monday? Mr. Busk announced a driving contest and handed out some flyers about it. When I took one, my classmates burst out laughing. Laughing!

None of this would be happening if we still lived in the city. I wouldn't even have to learn how to drive — ever! I'd just take buses and subways.

Whose idea was it to move to Port Lincoln, anyway?

NOT MINE!

Dad asked me again if I would mow the lawn today. HA! I said no way, José. We've only been here three weeks and he's *already* forgotten the agreement. I move to Long Island without complaining if I never have to mow a lawn or walk a dog.

That'll last, oh, a month or two. (No such word as "never" in this family!)

Might as well live it up while I can, huh?

Rachel did not write today. I could die waiting for a letter from her. I had no mail at all. No one from New York misses me. Just tons of catalogs for the Lorillards. One of them actually said, FREE GIFT FOR YOUR NEW HOME.

Well, they only lived here for two months. It *was* a new home for them.

I wonder why they moved.

Also, we got something else for the Trang family (the ones who lived here before the Lorillards).

I still get the creeps when I think of them. I told Mom today I thought it was bad luck to move into a house where somebody died. She just smiled and said he didn't die *in* the house. Duh. Nat thinks it's cool. He keeps saying he hears a beating heart under the floorboards, like in "The Tell-Tale Heart." He says *that* was why the Lorillards moved.

Was *I* such a jerk at twelve?

I don't think so.

Okay, here's my big confession of the day. I, Kirsten Wilkes, actually decided I liked the suburbs for a few minutes. I think it's because I'm getting to know this girl, Maria Sirocco, at school. She's practically the first person who said a word to me this whole three weeks! She has this thick, gorgeous, jet-black hair, and she wears the coolest clothes. She's kind of a loudmouth, but she's funny and nice. I think we're going to be friends. Yeah! She has a boyfriend named Virgil. He has short brown hair, braces, and glasses. Smart, I think. And quiet (unlike Maria). But he seems like a nice guy.

So there is hope, after all.

Now if only I didn't have to take driver's ed.

Chapter 2

Kirsten Wilkes sat silently in the backseat of the driver's ed car. Next to her, Sara Gartman exhaled with boredom. Gwen Mitchell was reading a magazine and chewing fruity-smelling gum on the other side of Sara.

Up front, Maria Sirocco began pulling the steering wheel to the right.

"Signal," Mr. Busk rasped from the passenger seat.

Some voice. Like he cleaned his vocal cords with a bottle brush.

Mr. Busk thought he was still in the Marines. At least it seemed that way. And despite his potbelly and receding hairline, he looked fit enough to storm a beachhead, or whatever Marines did. Rumor had it he lost his voice in the Vietnam War, along with some of his sanity. When he returned, he kind of snapped —

left his wife and disappeared for a few years. Then he came back and the school happily hired him to be a driver's ed and auto shop teacher.

Anyway, that was Maria's version of the story. Of course, Maria also said Mr. Busk used napalm for an aftershave.

The back of Mr. Busk's neck reminded Kirsten of rare roast beef. Pinkish-red, juicy, marbled with white lines. His short brown hair was stiff and sparse, like cut grass in a drought. You could scour pans by turning them upside down and rubbing them on his head.

. Bottle brush, napalm, roast beef, dry grass, scouring pad. Mm, what a guy.

Kirsten must have been grinning, because when Mr. Busk turned around, he said, "I'm glad you find this amusing, Kirsten. Now come up front and entertain the rest of us."

Oops. Maria had parked already. Sara and Gwen had taken their turns before Maria. Kirsten was the last driver today.

She opened the door and got out. Maria was standing there, waiting. "You'll be great," she said with a smile.

From inside the car a voice chirped, "Pray for your life."

"Cram it, Gwen," Maria called out. Then

she whispered to Kirsten, "Don't worry. I've got my gym bag. If she starts gasping like the last time, I'll stuff a sweat sock down her throat."

"Right." Kirsten forced a nervous laugh. She sank into the driver's seat as Maria got in back.

With a sigh, Kirsten fastened her seat belt. Oh, well, at least it was last period. If she got into an accident, they could all go to the hospital without missing any classes.

"Okay, Kristen," Mr. Buok said, "ease onto the street. Then take us back to the school."

"*Kir*sten."

"Kirsten. That's what I meant. Go."

Three weeks, and he was still having trouble with the name. Was "Kirsten" that unusual?

Turn key. Depress gas pedal.

How would he feel if she called him Mr. *Bust?* Mr. *Dust? Tusk?*

Foot on brake. Shift to Drive.

Alcohol. She could smell it. Just faintly.

Mr. *Soused.* That would be more like it.

Foot on gas pedal. Gently turn steering wheel to the left . . .

Screeeeeeeek!

The car tore away from the curb. Kirsten felt her body lurch backward against the seat.

"Owwww," moaned Sara.

"Easy!" Mr. Busk barked. "You got lead weights in your shoe?"

Kirsten lifted her foot and everyone jerked forward.

Gwen was giggling. Sara was sucking her teeth in disgust. Mr. Busk stared stonily ahead.

Kirsten felt about two inches tall. She wanted to drive the car over a cliff and forget about the whole thing.

Instead she pressed her foot lightly on the pedal and gripped the steering wheel so hard, her arms hurt. As she eased into the right lane, a pickup whooshed by. Someone inside it let out a wolf whistle. Kirsten's concentration faltered.

Intersection ahead. Just over the railroad tracks. Gate is up, light is green. *Yeah!* One left turn, and she'd be on the road to school.

The light turned to yellow.

Slow down.

Kirsten put her foot on the brake.

Honnnnnnnk!

A huge, angry-looking front grille snarled at Kirsten through the rearview mirror.

Her breath caught in her throat. She stepped on the gas. The car shot over the train tracks and toward the intersection as the light flicked to red.

"It's red it's red it's red *it's red*!" Gwen gasped in the backseat.

The car skidded to a stop, its engine groaning. Mr. Busk's back was arched. His foot was pressing down *his* brake, which was connected by a long metal bar to Kirsten's.

Mr. Busk unclenched his teeth. "Would you get your foot off the gas, please?"

Kirsten did, and the engine groan stopped.

"Oh my lord . . ." Sara muttered.

Mr. Busk was massaging his forehead. "Kirsten, when the light turns green, take us back *alive*, will you?"

Sweat formed an itchy ring beneath Kirsten's hairline. She approached Port Lincoln High School at seventeen miles per hour.

"Way to go," encouraged Maria softly from behind.

"Uh, can we get there to*day*, thank you very much?" Gwen remarked.

Thud.

"Ow! Maria hit me!"

Mr. Busk ignored them. Kirsten smiled as she signaled to turn into the school driveway.

Classes had already ended. Kids were leaning against cars, sitting on the stoop, walking, laughing, enjoying the crisp early-autumn air.

Relief washed over Kirsten. All she had to do was go through the gate, follow a wide driveway along the side of the school, and park in the big lot behind the building. End of lesson.

She turned right, steering toward the open gate. Out of the corner of her eye, she saw two students walking arm in arm toward the driveway. Of course they would see her and stop.

They smiled at each other. They kissed. They stepped off the curb together.

Right in front of Kirsten.

"Ohhh . . ."

She yanked the wheel to the left. She lifted her foot to step on the brake.

She missed.

Her foot clomped down on the gas pedal. The car tore off through the gate.

It careened up the driveway. Two football-player types dove into a hedge, their books flying. Kirsten executed a perfect ninety-degree skid into the parking lot.

Just beyond the lot, a pickup baseball game stopped as the players turned to watch.

Kirsten gritted her teeth. She was in control again. More or less. The front of the car was pointing right at the driver's ed parking spaces. Just to the right of the auto shop.

A group of kids had been working on an old, jacked-up car. Now they were staring at Kirsten in terror.

All of them scrambled around the car as she got closer.

All but one.

He was tall and dark-haired. His face was extremely bony. That was all Kirsten noticed before he took a step toward her approaching car.

"Watch it!" Mr. Busk bellowed.

"Oh oh oh oh oh oh oh!" Gwen gasped.

Kirsten and Mr. Busk jammed their feet on the brakes.

EEEEEEEEEEEEEE.

Thump.

With a dull cry, the boy fell to the blacktop.

Chapter 3

"Aaah! Aaah! Aaah! Aaah! Aaah! Aaah! Aaah!"

Gwen's rapid-fire shrieking filled the car as Kirsten pushed the door open.

The boy was sprawled on his back, eyes closed. Kirsten stared at the oil-stained T-shirt that showed under his black leather jacket. He wasn't breathing.

Mr. Busk barged through the gathering crowd. "Out of the way!"

Quickly he knelt down next to the boy and felt his pulse.

Maria and Sara stood beside Kirsten, stiff with shock. Gwen was staggering out of the car, bone-white. Her shrieks had become whimpers, and she was nervously fingering a locket around her neck.

Mr. Busk tilted the boy's head back until his mouth opened, then lowered himself to perform mouth-to-mouth resuscitation.

The boy's eyes sprang open.

"Yo," he said, looking into Mr. Busk's face. "I didn't know you cared."

Absolute silence. The crowd gaped, dumbfounded.

The guy stood up with a grin and brushed himself off. "I mean, really, you ain't my type, Mr. Busk."

From behind the old car, a whoop of laughter rang out. A couple of auto shop classmates stepped around the car and exchanged high fives with the boy.

"That was a *joke*?" Sara remarked.

Maria looked disgusted. "I can't believe this."

Gwen propped herself on the driver's ed car and covered her face with her hands.

Kirsten kept staring. She thought she had killed him. Her terror was slowly leaking out of her, like air through a pinhole in a tire.

He had *pretended*. He had scared half the school to death — for a dumb laugh. What kind of jerk would do something like that?

Mr. Busk stood up slowly. His fists were clenched. The veins in his temples stood out. The roast beef was becoming raw.

As he walked toward the boy, the crowd fell silent. Kids began to scatter.

But the guy wasn't backing away.

He was smirking. His green-gray eyes hadn't the slightest fear.

They were cold, steady, penetrating. The color of polished jade.

As he gave a casual glance across the crowd, his gaze met Kirsten's for an instant. A split-second, really. She wasn't sure he had even focused on her.

But Kirsten was rooted to the ground. Transfixed. In that instant she felt he had drunk her in, absorbed her like a sponge. She felt it in the follicles of her hair and the soles of her feet.

Kirsten had never seen eyes like that.

The spell was broken by Mr. Busk's voice. *"I want you out of my class, Maxson!"*

"Heyyy, come on, I was just kidding — "

As Mr. Busk roared in anger, Maria grabbed Kirsten by the arm. "Let's go," she said.

They began walking toward the driveway. Around them, the lot had emptied. Mr. Busk and the boy were face to face.

And the boy still had that cocky grin.

Mr. Busk's shouts faded as Kirsten and Maria approached the front of the school. "Who *was* that guy?" Kirsten asked.

Maria shot her a look. "Kirsten Wilkes, don't even *think* of it."

"Think of what?"

"Don't play dumb with me. Rob Maxson is a scuzzball. A slug. Pour salt on him and he shrivels up. Definitely NYT."

"NYT? *New York Times?*"

"Not Your Type."

Kirsten giggled. "Oh, I *know* that. It's just that . . . well, I mean, his *eyes* — "

"Yeah. Green. The color of slime. Need I say more?" Maria sighed. "Kirsten. Look what happened to Gwen. She used to be *nice* before she met him."

"They went out together?"

"Until he totally ruined her life."

"How?"

"He got bored with her and broke up. She was *devastated*. Well, for months Nguyen Trang had been mooning over her — so she went out with him, thinking Rob would get jealous. Nguyen showered her with gifts, gave her jewelry, treated her *sooo* specially. But she still loved Rob, and Nguyen knew it. That was why he did what he did. . . ." Maria's voice trailed off.

"What exactly *did* Nguyen do?" Kirsten asked. "All I know is that he was killed in a car accident."

"Well, that was the official report," Maria replied. "But everybody knows it wasn't really an accident."

Kirsten's eyes widened. "You mean, someone — "

"Not someone. Himself." Maria gave her a confidential look and lowered her voice. "He stole a car, Kirsten, and drove it into a ravine. He committed suicide."

Chapter 4

Suicide.

The word was so *ugly*. How could Nguyen Trang have done that? Over *Gwen*? What a waste.

Kirsten had a sudden pang of sympathy for Gwen. Imagine how she felt.

But if it were true — if Nguyen did commit suicide over her — hadn't *she* caused it by manipulating him?

What a horrible story. Why hadn't Kirsten known about it until now? She was living in the Trangs' old house. Why hadn't the Lorillards mentioned what had happened? Or the real-estate agent who had sold them the house?

Zing!

The Lightbulb of Obvious Answers switched on in Kirsten's head. Of course they didn't talk about it. How would the truth have sounded?

You'll love this house, Dr. Wilkes! Three bedrooms, two baths, new kitchen, nice location, and a recent suicide committed by one of the former residents!

Maria's face broke into a sudden smile. "Hey!" she called out. "Over here!"

Virgil Garth was standing in front of the school, looking bored. When he saw Maria he brightened. "Where were you?"

"You didn't hear?" Maria asked.

"Hear what?" Virgil said.

"Oh, Rob was being a sadistic jerk," Maria replied. Then, with a sly smile, she added, "But you'll never guess who has a crush on him."

"Mariaaaaa!" Kirsten felt the blood rushing to her face. She barely *knew* Virgil!

"Oh, come on, it's okay," Maria said. "Virgil had a crush on him, too."

Virgil grimaced. "Maria, what did you have in your lunch today?"

"Well, you used to think he was *soooo* cool."

"Yeah, but that's not the same as — "

Maria threw her arms around him. "I have a big mouth, but he loves me, anyway." She planted a kiss on Virgil's lips, and he blushed. "Go ahead," she continued, *"you* tell her about Rob."

Virgil rolled his eyes. "Well, he's kind of . . . unpredictable. If I were you — "

"You *guys*!" Kirsten interrupted. "I mean, I've never even *met* this guy."

"Keep it that way!" Maria said with a laugh. As she and Virgil began walking away, she said over her shoulder, "Call me later!"

"Okay."

Kirsten was amazed. Maria could say whatever was on her mind, no matter how obnoxious — but you couldn't stay angry with her.

She watched Maria and Virgil for a while, then headed in the other direction, toward her house.

This was one part of suburban life she liked. Walking home among the chirping birds, shuffling through bright piles of fresh-fallen leaves, smelling the cool, sweet air. It was a far cry from the sweat, the B.O., and the car-horn noise of her ride home on the M19 crosstown bus.

Each day Kirsten was missing New York City less. Port Lincoln wasn't so bad. Despite the cliques. And the fact that kids went everywhere in cars. And hung out at a mall. And wore the same clothes. From the same store.

Well, almost all the kids were like that. Rob wasn't. How had Virgil described him?

Unpredictable.

Virgil had used that word so *dramatically*, as if it were the world's worst quality. No kidding, Rob was unpredictable. Kirsten had seen that, all right.

But behind that word was something else. Rob was different. Different in dress, attitude, looks.

Different from *us*.

And being different was deadly in Port Lincoln.

Kirsten laughed to herself. *Now* who was being dramatic?

She walked down Anchor Street to her family's white, Cape-Cod-style house. With the overgrown lawn and the mismatched curtains.

Kirsten was kind of proud of the fact that her house stuck out. The Wilkeses were in no great hurry to be exactly like everybody else. The walls of the house were still bare, save for one enormous china platter that her mom had hung on the kitchen wall because it wouldn't fit anywhere else.

From the outside the house was dark and still, all the doors and windows locked. Precautions left over from city living. Never give a burglar a chance. Kirsten bounded up the stairs, key in hand. She grabbed the mail from the box, which still bore a brass plaque with THE LORILLARD'S stamped on it, misplaced apostrophe and all.

Clutching the stack of letters, Kirsten let herself in.

The house was dark, clammy. After the fragrant walk home, the stale air was suffocating. Kirsten went to open a window.

Then she stopped.

Someone was in the house.

She didn't know how she knew it. But she did.

"Hello?"

No answer.

"Nat?"

This had happened last week. She'd come home to an empty house and Nat had sprung out of the kitchen pantry, scaring her to death.

"Don't do this to me, Nat!"

Kirsten thought a moment. It was the last Tuesday of the month. That meant Dad was at the hospital seeing Emergency Room patients, Mom was at her monthly editorial board meeting — and Nat had soccer practice. That was it.

She walked into the kitchen, plopped the mail on the table, and let her backpack fall to the floor.

The windowless, L-shaped pantry was dark. She pulled the light switch and looked inside. Just to be sure.

It was empty.

She carefully opened the door to the back foyer and hung her jacket on a wall hook.

To the right of the hooks was the door to the basement. She opened it and peered down the stairs.

"Hello?"

Natless.

She was alone. Safe.

No, I'm not.

Why did she still have that feeling?

It was the house.

Had to be. It always felt a little like a locker room. Even on a beautiful, balmy day like this. Too much insulation, maybe. Her family would just have to learn to leave a few windows open when they left.

Which is just what she did, before heading straight for the fridge.

In moments she put together a nice, thick, toasted cinnamon-raisin bagel with a huge wad of cream cheese in the middle. Her favorite snack. Guaranteed to cure all ills.

As she munched away, she flipped through the mail. Not one envelope had her name on it.

22

That did it. She vowed to write her ex-best friend Rachel Ross out of her will. She would *make* a will just to do that.

If Rachel had written a letter, Kirsten could be reading it now. Then she could have written back. What a great afternoon it would have been.

Now, instead, she had to do her homework.

She reached into her backpack and pulled out its contents. Social studies text (yawn), math book (gross), French lesson (*quel ennui*), and a stack of dog-eared papers — notes, mimeographs, whatever.

Kirsten glanced at the glossy sheet on top. It was the driving-contest flyer Mr. Busk had given her class the week before.

Kirsten felt a knot in her stomach. The kids had laughed when she'd taken it. She had been so embarrassed, she had stuck it in her pack and never read it.

WIN THE CAR OF YOUR DREAMS! was emblazoned across the top. Under that were the contest rules:

1. All PLHS seniors in driver's ed classes are eligible.
2. The winner must have the highest com-

bined scores on his or her written test and road test.

3. Tie scores will be decided by lottery.
4. Top prize is on view at CUNNINGHAM MOTORS of Port Lincoln.

In the center of the flyer was a color photo, the sleek profile of a white Ford Escort, speeding along a highway.

Ha! Fat chance, Wilkes, Kirsten said to herself. She folded the flyer and stuck it back in her pack.

Eeny, meeny, miney, mo. Social studies first.

She opened her book. After one paragraph, her eyes began to wander.

Across the table, the stack of mail had fallen over. The letters had fanned across the table, right to the edge. Kirsten stooped to pick up one that had dropped to the floor.

Actually, it was only a piece of an envelope.

It must have fallen out of her hands when she came in — but where was the rest of it?

Kirsten looked closer. She could make out half a postmark, with strange, foreign letters — and below it, the letter *M*, where the address should begin.

She retraced her steps back to the mailbox.

Nothing had fallen onto the living room carpet.

The missing pieces were outside — two at the bottom of the mailbox, one in a corner of the porch, and the rest under the bushes in front of the house.

She brought them inside, muttering to herself. Her dad *loved* to complain about the post office, especially when they sent those little plastic bags with destroyed letters inside and a computer-printed apology. The letters always looked as if they had been chewed by a wild tiger.

Maybe they didn't use plastic bags in the suburbs. But the tigers were much fiercer.

These pieces were *shredded*, not ripped. They looked as if they'd been in an explosion.

A letter-bomb, she thought. Maybe that was what she should send to Rachel.

Taking a roll of tape from the kitchen desk drawer, she began piecing the fragments of the envelope together, like a jigsaw puzzle.

The address on the envelope soon came together:

Mr. and Mrs. H. Trang
477 Anchor Street
Port Lincoln, New York 11500

The return address read, Outreach, Inc., Ho Chi Minh City, Vietnam.

Kirsten was used to seeing junk mail for the Lorillards and Trangs, but this was definitely not junk mail.

She got to work on the letter, which was typed on onionskin paper with an old-fashioned typewriter.

As the letter began to form, a tiny voice began to pipe up in back of her head: *This is none of your business.*

But it was her business. What if the letter was about a huge inheritance? Or a note from a long-lost relative? What if the Trangs had to go to Vietnam right away for some emergency?

Do we have the Trangs' address? she wondered. She doubted it. The Lorillards wouldn't have left it, nor the real-estate agent. They'd acted as though the Trangs never existed.

And that was just plain wrong.

Kirsten owed it to the Trangs to forward this letter.

Not all the pieces were there, but slowly the message began to take shape:

Dear Mr. and Mrs. Trang,
    Outreach Americ

uniting family members of the Southeast Asian-American community with lost or forgotten loved ones overseas.
I   task filled with sublime joy and, sometimes, unexpected sadness.
          unately, in the latter spirit that we must inform you that Mr. and Mrs. R. Haing, the parents of your nephew, Nguyen, have been located. Last month they died of natural causes. Please accept o   of deepest sorrow for you and the young man.

In Sympathy,
Lynn Ngor
Director

Nguyen was a refugee. He had dropped his real last name, taken his uncle's. Or had he been sent here as a child? Did he *know* about his parents?

Kirsten turned another piece of the letter over.

This one had a stain on it.

A dark, red stain. Still wet.

Chapter 5

"Hello? . . . *Stop!* . . . Hello? . . . Will you — ?"

"Hi, Maria?" Kirsten said into the receiver. "It's Kirsten. I have to talk to you!"

"Down, Virgil! Hi!" Maria burst into giggles. Kirsten could hear barking noises in the background. "Sorry. Virgil thinks it's hilarious to distract me when I'm on the phone. *Virgil, it's my father!*"

The barking stopped.

"There. Now, what's up?"

"Do either of you know where Nguyen Trang's family moved?"

"Hang on." Her voice became muffled and distant as she asked Virgil the same question. "Uh-uh. Neither of us knew him that well. Why?"

"I need to swear you to secrecy about something." Kirsten told her everything — about the letter, the condition she had found it in, the stain.

"Whoa. Gross," was Maria's reaction. "Maybe the mailman got attacked by a dog, and held the letter out — "

"None of my neighbors has a dog."

"A cat? A killer gerbil?"

"It's not funny, Maria. Who would do something like this? I mean, what if the Trangs were, like, spies, and someone is looking through our mail? Who knows what else they'll do?"

"Hey, chill, Kirsten. The war ended before we were born. The letter probably got chewed up by some machine at the post office. The stain could be anything — mud, a squashed berry, bird droppings. Be real. Just write 'Please forward' on the envelope and leave it for the mail carrier to take. They forward the rest of the personal mail, right? Or do you get all of the Trangs' letters?"

"No, just some junk mail," Kirsten replied.

"Okay, so problem solved. That'll be forty-five dollars, please."

Kirsten took a deep breath. "I don't know, Maria, I — I just feel creepy in this house. *You* know. I always have. And now that you told me about Nguyen's death — "

"Ugh. The haunted house business again."

"*Nooo!* I didn't say I — "

"Look, Kirsten, if it makes you rest easier, everybody knows cremated people do not come back as ghosts."

"*Ghosts?* Maria, I don't — this is *dumb.* . . ." Kirsten paused. "Nguyen was cremated? How do you know?"

"It was in all the local papers. Kirsten, Nguyen's death was the biggest news item in Port Lincoln in years. When the Trangs went to sprinkle the ashes around the crash site, Mr. Trang had to push photographers out of the way."

"How come nobody ever talks about it?"

"I don't know. I guess it's one of those things people like to forget. And *nobody* really knew the Trangs well. They kept to themselves. Nguyen was, like, a shadow. He blended into the walls at school. I do know he liked cars, though."

"Enough to steal one?"

"Who knows? He was a little weird. He was into magic and . . . that *thing*, what's it called? You know, where you move things just by thinking about them? Maybe he thought he could make the car fly."

"Come on," Kirsten said. "Do people really think — "

"*Telekinesis*," Maria cut in.

"Huh?"

"That's what it's called. Like in the book, *Carrie*. Whatever. It was a joke. The point is, Nguyen wasn't in his right mind, Kirsten. He was upset. Suicidal — over *Gwen*, if you can imagine that. I mean, his aunt and uncle insisted he *couldn't* have done it. They said he would never even steal a piece of gum." Maria sighed sadly. "But what did they know about love, right? It was obvious he did it. The car belonged to this old guy — you know, Olaf, who walks around town talking to himself? Anyway, he *saw* Nguyen take it. And when the wreckage was found, Nguyen's body was the only one in it."

"Maybe someone else stole it, and forced him to go along," Kirsten suggested.

"That's what the Trangs said," Maria replied. "But the cops couldn't get fingerprints, because everything was burned."

"Ohhhh . . ." Kirsten felt her stomach turn.

"And besides," Maria continued, "Nguyen was in the driver's seat."

The phone went silent for a moment.

"How . . . awful," was all Kirsten could think to say.

"Yeah. It got worse, too. The poor Trangs. They started out making these polite, sad statements to the press. But they slowly went nuts — insisting there was a conspiracy, prejudice against Asians, he was kidnapped, blah, blah, blah. They kept saying they would find Nguyen's diary, and that would give all the clues to what really happened."

"And then they just gave up?"

"Well, all these movie and TV people started showing up at their house, trying to get the rights to their story, and that pushed them over the edge. Last June they finally just moved. They said they were devastated and wanted to live out their lives anonymously."

"End of story."

"Yeah." Maria laughed. "Hey, maybe those producers are sneaking around your house, fighting over the Trangs' mail."

Actually, *that* didn't seem far-fetched to Kirsten.

"Listen," Maria went on, "Virgil's getting lonely. I better go. Don't worry."

"Yeah, okay. I'll see you tomorrow."

"Bye."

"Bye."

Kirsten hung up and slumped back into the kitchen seat. It was definitely time to lighten up. Send the letter on and stop worrying.

She took a red pen and wrote ADDRESSEE MOVED. PLEASE —

She stopped when she heard the creaking.

Eeeeeeeeeeee . . .

She put the pen down. It was coming from the porch.

Kirsten swallowed. Slowly she got up from the chair and walked toward the kitchen entrance.

"Kirrrrrrr-sssten . . ."

The voice was low and growly.

In the dining room.

Just past the kitchen door.

Kirsten froze. Her hands shaking, she reached for the letter opener on the table.

Then, with a blood-curdling shriek, a hooded figure leaped into the kitchen.

Chapter 6

"Aaaaaaaaah — !" Kirsten screamed.

But she swallowed it.

Her attacker was on the floor, laughing. Holding a piece of paper that had been folded into a cone, like a megaphone.

Kirsten caught her breath. The feeling was beginning to return to her extremities.

And anger to her brain.

"I hate you, Nat," Kirsten snapped. "You are a total, hateful, worthless dork."

"Whatever you say bounces off me and sticks to you!" Nat replied.

"And immature, too!"

Kirsten stormed off and wished her mom had given birth to a toad twelve years ago.

Then again, maybe she had.

*   *   *

Rrrrrrrommmm . . . rrrrrrrommmmm!

Kirsten and Maria were early for driver's ed on Wednesday. As they waited for everyone else, they watched the auto shop class busily testing the car they were working on. Someone inside it was gunning the accelerator while another two had their heads in the engine. The rest of the class stood by, nodding knowingly.

"Why do boys like cars so much?" Kirsten asked.

"One word: testosterone," Maria said. "Named after a famous Italian scientist, Giovanni Testosterone. It is secreted by the hormonal gland and makes males interested in loud, pollution-causing objects and unable to follow a beat on a dance floor. You can look it up."

Kirsten laughed. The boys were arguing about something over the drone of the engine — gravely tossing around words she had never heard, as if the future of the world depended on it.

The car's front door opened. The guy in the driver's seat had been hidden behind dark-tinted windows. Now Kirsten could see it was Rob.

As he casually stepped out and shut the door

behind him, he seemed worlds away from the grubby, yammering guys around the hood. He was no Tom Cruise, that was for sure, but he had something the others didn't have. A coolness, a sureness — a *grace*. He, Kirsten knew, would be able to follow a beat on a dance floor.

This time, when his eyes met Kirsten's, they stopped. Before she could look away, she saw the expression change on his face.

He smiled.

No doubt about it. He had remembered her from yesterday.

The smile sent a chill through Kirsten — cool, sharp, almost icy. She felt stung. Shivery. She wasn't sure she liked it.

But she wasn't sure she didn't.

When she looked back, he was hunched over the engine with the others. They were hanging on his every word.

"Okay, let's look lively!"

Mr. Busk was trotting toward the driver's ed car. Gwen had already climbed into the front seat, Maria and Sara into the back.

Kirsten ran to the back door, but Sara pulled it shut. "Would you mind using the other side? I'm tired of sitting on the hump."

"Oh. Okay," Kirsten replied. She raced around to the other door.

As she was getting in, she heard a distant low-pitched chuckle.

She looked over to see Rob, watching her with a grin. This time she returned the smile.

When Kirsten sat down, Maria glared at her. "Ah-hem. I saw that."

"Stop," Kirsten said, rolling her eyes.

Gwen took off a bit suddenly. She steered the car out of the lot and past the school.

"Turn left," Mr. Busk growled.

"You bet," Gwen chirped.

"Cross Sunrise and make your first right."

"Okey-dokey."

Gwen signaled, made full stops at the stop signs, accelerated and decelerated gently, and made pleasant chitchat with Mr. Busk.

When Gwen was done, she parallel-parked perfectly and thanked Mr. Busk for his pointers.

"No problem," Mr. Busk replied. "You're my easiest student." Over his shoulder, he said, "I don't know, girls, I think we got a front runner for that Escort."

"Oh, please," Maria muttered.

Kirsten wanted to puke.

Sara took her turn next.

As Gwen climbed into the backseat, she was smiling triumphantly. A *just-try-to-beat-that* kind of smile.

After Sara, Kirsten drove. She ran a stop sign, bumped the curb on a wide turn, and was cursed at by one driver. Mr. Busk said he was pleased at the improvement.

Later, walking away from class with Maria, Kirsten felt morose. "I swear, I will never learn to drive."

"Well, Kirsten, let's face it — you will probably *not* win the contest," Maria replied. "But between you and me, that's okay. What Gwen doesn't realize is that the winner of the Escort has to marry Mr. Busk."

"Gross!"

"You'll get the hang of it. Don't worry. Everybody does. My *grandmother*, who grew up in the city like you, learned how to drive at age fifty."

"Now I'm inspired," Kirsten said dryly. *"I'll* do it by forty-nine."

"That's the spirit!"

At their usual turn-off spot in front of the school, they said good-bye.

Kirsten hadn't gotten a half block away before she heard a car horn blowing "Taps."

She turned to see an old, beat-up Mustang on oversized wheels. "Want a ride?" called a deep, throaty voice.

Rob was inside. He was leaning clear across

the seat to talk to her through the passenger window — and was still driving straight.

Alligator eyes. That's what they were like, Kirsten decided. She had once seen a photo of an alligator-filled swamp at night. The photo was almost pitch-black, except for what looked like tiny pairs of floating green fireballs. That was how you knew alligators were there.

"Um . . . yeah, I guess," Kirsten answered.

He pulled up to the curb and stopped. The car was a wreck. Rob was moving the soda cans, magazines, and plastic wrappers from the passenger bucket seat and tossing them in the back. Billows of shredded foam stuck out of the seat's ripped seams. Rob quickly covered them with an old T-shirt he took off the floor. "Come on in."

He's got to be kidding, Kirsten thought. *He expects me to sit on that?*

"The shirt's clean," he said. "Don't worry."

Oh. Well. In that case. Kirsten pulled open the door.

She took a quick look behind her. Maria was a block away, staring in intense disapproval.

With a shrug and a guilty smile, Kirsten sat in the car.

It was a *ride*, for God's sake, not an elopement.

Maria would get over it.

The T-shirt bunched down around the small of her back, but Kirsten didn't mind. "Thanks," she said.

"No problem." He glided to a smooth stop at a red light.

He was a *very* good driver.

Kirsten sneaked a look at him as he watched the light. His brows were dark and coffee-brown, slanting upward, chiseling his forehead with neat parallel lines of concern.

"I'm Rob Maxson," he said, still staring straight ahead.

"Kirsten Wilkes."

"Hm. Nice name." Rob made a right turn onto Merrick Road, then a quick left onto Burnside. "I . . . I'm sorry for that trick I pulled on you yesterday. I hope I didn't scare you too much."

"Well, it was a little . . . scary."

Ugh. Nothing like disagreeing, and not even finding original words to do it with.

Rob nodded. "I can be a jerk sometimes. A crazy idea pops into my head, and something gets into me. I say, 'Go for it' without thinking. I don't know why."

"That's okay." Kirsten was impressed. Boys and apologies usually didn't go together.

Especially boys like Rob. This was a nice surprise. "I get that way, too. I mean, I'm here, right?"

Rob's laughter was sudden and explosive. "Riding with me *is* a crazy idea, that's true."

Kirsten realized something. "Do you have a license?"

"Yeah. I turned seventeen in June, and I took my test this summer. Mr. Busk's an old buddy — well, he *was*, anyway — and he gave me free private lessons."

"Lucky you."

"He had to. He owed me a favor."

Rob didn't explain. Kirsten had the strong feeling she shouldn't pursue it.

They rode silently down Anchor Street, until Rob pulled up into Kirsten's driveway. "Well, nice getting to know you," he said.

"Me, too." Kirsten squeezed the door handle, then stopped. "Hey, how did you know where I lived?"

"Oh! Uh . . ." A look flashed across Rob's face, blank and inward. Then, slowly, he turned away with a sheepish smile. "I saw you out front . . . last week, mowing the lawn. I guess you stayed in my mind."

Kirsten felt herself turning hot. He was lying — well, sort of. She had never mowed this lawn. But what was the difference? He probably saw her doing something else. "Well, thanks for the ride," she said, squeezing the door handle to let herself out. "Um, I'd invite you in, but no one's home."

"Oh, yeah?" Rob's eyes lit up.

Kirsten felt a jolt of fear. *Why did you say that, you fool?* she said to herself. *You don't know him. You don't know what he wants.*

"Then let's switch," Rob added.

"What?"

"Switch. You drive and I coach."

"Oh, I don't know. . . ."

"Why not? You don't want to go into an empty house, right? Besides, I'm a better teacher than Mr. Busk."

"I'm sure you are, but I *stink*, Rob. I already crashed my dad's car."

Rob quickly got out and walked around to the passenger side. "May I have your jacket, please?" he asked in a mock British accent.

Coming from Rob, this sounded ridiculous. "My *jacket*?" Kirsten asked with a giggle.

"It's warm. We want you comfortable and free to move your arms."

"Oh, *okay*." Kirsten reluctantly got out, gave him her jacket, and dragged herself to the other side. "I hope this car is insured," she muttered.

She slid in, then nervously went through each necessary step: *Put on seat belt. Adjust mirrors. Pump the gas a few times. Start engine.*

Rawwwr . . . rawwwr . . . rawwwr. . . . It wouldn't catch.

"Uh, you flooded the engine," Rob said. "You gave it too much gas. Try starting it with your foot off the gas."

Kirsten did what he said, and the engine started perfectly. Immediately she began backing up.

"Kirsten," Rob said softly, "always look over your shoulder before you back out. Don't trust your mirrors."

With one hand on the steering wheel, Kirsten turned to look behind her as the car rolled backward.

Into her line of vision, from behind a hedge, rode a small girl on a bike with training wheels.

Kirsten screamed. Her foot slipped off the accelerator and flailed aimlessly.

"*Susan!*" shrieked a woman's voice.

The little girl stopped behind the car and froze.

Chapter 7

Scrreeeeeeek!

Kirsten jammed her foot down so hard, her thigh ached.

The car jolted to a sudden stop.

The girl's mother swooped her daughter up off the bike. "Oh, thank God!" she said. "Susie, you *see* why you have to be careful?"

Kirsten's heart felt like a pounding sledgehammer. Her stomach clenched into a knot.

"Sorry!" the mother called out. "Thank you!"

Kirsten took a moment to catch her breath. "If I hadn't looked back," she managed to say, "I would have killed her."

Rob nodded. "You did great, Kirsten. Now you'll always know."

"I don't think I can go on."

"You have to now. Or you'll always be scared."

Kirsten collected herself and continued backing out, extremely slowly.

He saved that girl's life, Kirsten thought.

She was going to listen to everything he said.

Rob continued to give Kirsten directions as she drove through the streets of Port Lincoln. He encouraged her when she did well. He was patient and forgiving about her mistakes. Kirsten had no idea a gravelly voice could be so gentle.

Soon Kirsten's hands weren't shaking. On Sunrise Highway, which ran along the train tracks, she actually switched between lanes and no one blew a horn at her.

When Rob asked her to drive through the narrow U-shaped driveway of Dairy Land Take-Out, she did it without crashing into the metal poles on either side.

The clerk's smile fell as Kirsten drove past her without stopping. "Just passing through!" Rob yelled out.

Kirsten couldn't help laughing. "This is *fun.*"

"Okay, parking time," Rob said. "One free popcorn if you get the car between the lines in the multiplex parking lot."

"*Rob*, I can't see a movie now!"

"Not even one with Jason Priestley in it?"

"Well . . ." Kirsten *loved* Jason Priestley. "It is a Wednesday."

"Call your parents from a pay phone. My treat."

"The phone call?"

"I know. My generosity is amazing."

Kirsten carefully drove into the lot and maneuvered into a space. Rob opened the door and looked down at the printed parking lines.

"Did I make it?" Kirsten asked.

Rob grinned. "Butter or plain?"

"*Lots* of butter!" Kirsten practically shouted. She had done it! Driven without fear and without mistakes.

And it was all because of Rob. Rob the slug, Rob the scuzzball.

Rob, the nicest guy she had met in months.

"Kirsten, you are going to be the star of your class," Rob said.

"No way. Gwen Mitchell is — "

Oops. Kirsten had forgotten what Maria had said about Rob and Gwen. Big mistake to bring *her* up.

"Gwen? Forget her!" Rob leaned over the seat and rummaged through the trash in the back of the car. He pulled out a sheet of paper.

When he sat back down, Kirsten could see he was holding the contest flyer. He took a marker from the glove compartment and wrote KIRSTEN'S CAR across it. With a flourish, he drew a huge exclamation mark, with one of the Escort's headlights as its dot.

Kirsten laughed. "Get out of here."

Rob shrugged, folded it up, and put it in his jacket pocket. "You'll see. Now come on, call your 'rents." He handed her a quarter.

As Kirsten went straight to the pay phone, Rob headed for the ticket line. "Ask them if you can go to dinner, too!" he called out.

A date! This was an honest-to-God *date*!

Yeaaaah!

Kirsten's heart was running like a motor. She thought she'd have to wait till *college* to be asked out.

She got the answering machine at home.

"Hi, Mom? Dad?" she said in a cheery voice. "I'm out with . . . a friend. Don't worry about saving dinner for me. I'll see you all afterward. Bye."

Ugh. What a sneak. She knew she'd face the firing squad later on. Everything about this was wrong: a movie on a school night with a boy her parents would *hate*.

But, hey, you only live once.

Besides, even if Rob turned out to be boring, it *was* a Jason Priestley movie.

And if the movie was a dud, there was always popcorn.

The final score? Three for three.

Wonderful company. Phenomenal movie. Excellent popcorn.

Rob was quiet during the movie's sad parts, whispered a couple of funny comments during the boring section, and didn't hog the bucket.

They couldn't stop talking about the movie afterward, as they walked to the nearby Friendly's. There, Rob scrunched his eyebrows, turned up his collar, and did a *great* Jason Priestley imitation. Loudly. Girls began walking by their booth, staring at him, their mouths hanging open.

Rob was a terrific listener, too, sensitive and interested in Kirsten's life story. Dinner passed by in a flash, and Rob paid with a credit card. ("It's my mom's," he said. "You can get me next time.")

It wasn't until they'd left that Kirsten realized they had not talked about him.

They walked back to the car arm in arm. Kirsten nuzzled her head on his shoulder.

"Rob?" she said dreamily. "Who are you?"

Rob stiffened. "What do you mean?"

"I mean, we just spent four hours together, and I don't know the first thing about you — your family, what you like, *anything*."

After a long silence, they reached the car. "You want to drive?"

"Sure." Kirsten opened the door and sank into the front seat.

With a deep sigh, Rob sat next to her. "There's really nothing to talk about," he said.

Kirsten started up and backed out of the space. "I don't believe that. Why are you so shy about yourself?"

"It's just that — well, I haven't really gotten this close to a girl before." He paused, staring distantly at the dashboard. "I — I guess I'm a little ashamed, too. My mom . . . well, I don't see much of her. She works a lot, and she has some . . . I don't know, *problems*, I guess. My dad used to work at the shoe factory, but he lost his job. He and Mom started getting on each other's case. Then, one morning — "

He fell silent. The Mustang's brakes squeaked slightly as Kirsten stopped for a red light.

Finally Rob continued, in a voice barely above a whisper. "It was last April. I woke up and went downstairs. Mom was passed out on the floor. They'd stayed up all night, fighting and drinking. And Dad had run out. Haven't seen him since."

"I'm . . . sorry," Kirsten said softly.

Rob stared out the window for a long time. Finally he said, "Beautiful out, huh?"

"Yeah," Kirsten replied, looking at the nearly full moon.

As her eyes went back to the road, the light turned green and she accelerated. Suddenly she was gripped with fear — a fear she had always felt when she was behind a steering wheel.

But the fear was weak now, almost an obligation. It disappeared as quickly as it came.

She smiled. "Whoa. Rob, I just — *forgot* I was driving. It feels so natural."

"Hey, excellent," Rob said. "Want to try a parallel park? Then maybe we can get out and walk around?"

Kirsten had just passed the high school. To her right was the park. Cars were lined up at the curb.

Inside some of the cars, couples were making out. They were the ones who hadn't made it into the park yet.

Kirsten felt a shudder. It was late enough.

Her parents were going to kill her. And she was smart enough to know what an invitation into the park meant.

Everyone in school knew.

Rob's eyes were burning into her now. But they were softer than usual, glazed with tears.

"Rob? Are you okay?"

"Yeah. Sure. Um, look, I know what you're thinking. About the park. But it's such an incredible night. Just a walk, okay? I promise. You call the shots."

Kirsten flipped on her right signal and slowed down. "Okay."

The car ended up about a foot and a half from the curb. Not bad. It was progress.

Rob helped her on with her jacket. They strolled into the park and took a footpath that curved around the still, night-blackened duck pond. Cars were not allowed on the paths, and the loudest sound was the rustling of leaves overhead. For a long while, neither said a word. Kids sat on the surrounding benches, talking or just watching the moon reflect off the water.

Around the other side of the pond was a small, enclosed, wooded glade. Pathways wound through the stout maples and evergreens. The action on the benches here was much more serious. Couples were less likely to be talking. Or even upright.

"Maybe . . . we should turn around now," Kirsten said.

Rob smiled. "Okay, if you don't trust me."

"I *do*, but — "

"Then let's sit." Rob sank down onto a bench that had a view of the pond.

Kirsten took a deep breath. It would be all right. It would. Rob was okay. Mysterious, not totally truthful, but okay.

Besides, a good, loud scream could be heard by at least twenty people.

Rob picked up a pebble and threw it in the pond. Two sleepy ducks ruffled their feathers and swam away.

Kirsten sat next to him and tried to feel comfortable. Rob looked distant now, staring blankly across the water, as if she weren't there.

"Gorgeous, huh?" Kirsten offered.

Rob reached into his jacket pocket and pulled out a pack of cigarettes. Along with it came the folded-up contest flyer.

"Hey, look what I found," he said.

He opened it up. Kirsten smiled. KIRSTEN'S CAR! it said, blazing above the car's grille.

"Wishful thinking." Kirsten began to chuckle, but stopped.

Something was different.

Rob had drawn the dot of the exclamation mark as a big circle, around one of the headlights.

Now it was next to the headlight. Alone and open.

The car was angled toward them. Kirsten could see the entire grille. She was *sure* the Escort was in profile before. Or at least closer to a profile.

It was as if it had moved.

Kirsten thought of saying something, but it just seemed too ridiculous. She'd only glanced at the photo before. It was a trick of memory. That's all.

Besides, another question had popped into her head.

"Rob, if you already have your license, why do you have this flyer?"

"Um . . . Mr. Busk gave one to me. He knows I like Escorts."

Kirsten didn't believe it. She could tell by the hitch in his voice, a tightness around the eyelids. She was beginning to know him.

"Rob, I don't know how to say this, but, you can always be truthful to me."

"What do you mean?"

Kirsten looked him straight in the eye. "I don't mind driving with you, even if you don't have your license yet," she said firmly. "And another thing. I have never mowed my lawn, but I still like you."

"What?"

"You said you saw me mowing my lawn. That was how you knew where I lived."

Now Rob's entire face tightened. He looked toward the pond again, frowning, not saying a word.

Around them, couples were beginning to straggle out of the park. Kirsten realized it must be getting late.

Finally Rob said, "Okay. I confess. I've been checking you out since the first day of school. But I — I didn't want you to think I was chasing you."

"But that's *sweet*, Rob. You thought I wouldn't like you because you liked me?"

Rob turned to face her, openly, for the first time since they'd sat down. His eyes seemed to catch the full light of the moon, reflecting it back twice as brightly. "I guess I ought to just give in, huh, Kirsten?"

He drew closer.

Yes.

The eyes.

They were telling her what to do. Catching her in their electric neon brightness. Leading her like daylight at the end of a long, lonely tunnel.

His lips came nearer to hers, opening slowly.

Kirsten wanted to close her eyes, but couldn't.

Something was *off*.

Rob's arms were like steel clamps. He was pushing her down. Forcing her.

She was caught. She had no room to struggle.

Kirsten felt herself dropping beneath his weight. Then he closed his alligator eyes and she felt two cold folds of flesh close on her mouth.

Chapter 8

"Nnnnn — "

Kirsten pushed, but it was no use. She felt the cool condensation of the park bench against the back of her neck. Rob's lips pressed tightly against hers. Kirsten did the one thing she could think of.

She bit down.

"Yeeoooooowww!" Rob sprang back. He put his hand to his mouth in agony, letting go of the cigarettes and the contest flyer he had been clutching. A rivulet of blood trickled down his chin.

Kirsten picked herself up and backed away.

"I — I'm sorry! Are you okay?"

He removed his hand. In the soft moonlight, his lower lip and chin looked black with blood.

"Why dih oo doo at?" he moaned, his words slurry and agitated.

"Rob, you were forcing me — "

"*Forhing?*" Rob gagged on the blood. He coughed, cleared his throat, and spit. "I was doing what you wanted!"

"Doing what *I* wanted? How can you say that? You promised we'd take a *walk*!"

"We did take a walk! But then what happened, huh? I sat here, and what did *you* do? You didn't keep *walking*. You sat next to me. Didn't you, or am I crazy?"

Kirsten's sympathy drained out of her so fast, she could almost hear a sucking sound. "So that gave you permission to start wrestling me? Did you ever hear of asking?"

"What is this? I take you to the movies, pay for dinner, give you a driving lesson — "

"And now I'm supposed to do whatever you want? I don't believe this!" The anger was welling up from her chest, making her see red. She picked up the flyer from the ground, crumpled it into a ball, and threw it at him.

"Heyyy, easy!" he said, catching it.

"No, Rob," Kirsten shot back. "Not as easy as you think!"

She spun away and stormed out of the park. The two remaining couples, each of which had been happily entwined, were now sitting up.

They watched her leave, looking dumbfounded and annoyed.

Kirsten couldn't have cared less.

As she reached the sidewalk, she slowed down. She listened for footsteps. Of course Rob was going to come apologize. He wouldn't let her walk away. He'd made a big mistake, sure, but he was a nice guy underneath. She had seen that. Besides, it was late. And dark.

Finally Kirsten looked over her shoulder. The benches along the street side of the pond stood empty. A duck floated across the yellow streak of moonlight on the water. Beyond the pond, Kirsten saw only suggestions of shapes.

She thought of going back. Had she been too severe? Too judgmental? Too violent?

She paused to think. She grabbed her backpack out of Rob's car.

Then, with a sigh, she began the long walk home.

As she turned onto Burnside, Kirsten heard the roar of a car engine and hoped for a moment that Rob was chasing after her. But the noise died out instantly.

All she heard now were hints of sound. The rustling leaves, the distant overhead-wire hum, a ripple of laughter from a nearby house.

At the corner, someone was waiting. He was crouched behind a tree.

Eleven dollars. Right pocket. That's all I have. Take it. Kirsten mentally rehearsed her response. What were the things you were supposed to do? *Swing your arms crazily. Walk in the street. Sing "The Battle Hymn of the Republic" at the top of your lungs. Drool. Pick your nose.*

She veered into the street. *"MINE EYES HAVE SEEN — "*

He wasn't moving.

"THE GLORY OF THE — "

A light went on in the second-floor window of a house.

Abruptly she stopped singing.

The mugger was in full sight now.

He had four short legs and a shiny, curved head. The words U.S. MAIL were printed on his side.

A mailbox.

She groaned. Her friends in New York would be howling if they only knew.

In the lit window an old man scowled, then disappeared into a sudden snap of darkness.

Relax. Kirsten needed to relax. This wasn't the city. The streets were safe. People minded their business. You could walk after dark without worry. Here you didn't find pan-handlers, crime, filth, danger.

Or, unfortunately, cabs. She could use one right now.

The half mile to her house on Anchor Street was like a marathon. Nat's light was off up-stairs, which made her heart sink. If he was already asleep, it was late.

And she was in big trouble.

As she padded up her driveway, she reached into her jacket pocket for the keys.

It was empty except for a headband and some wrappers.

She tried her pants pocket. She rummaged through her backpack, trying not to let anything rattle.

By now she was at the back door. She peered inside. The small foyer between the door and the kitchen was dark.

Where had she put them? She retraced the evening in her mind. They were in her jacket, yes. That much she was sure of. She had taken her jacket off to drive —

And given it to Rob. In front of the house.

Maybe the keys fell into the gutter when he took the jacket. She turned toward the drive-way and began tiptoeing back.

And a heavy hand landed on her shoulder.

Chapter 9

Kirsten thought her heart would jump through her mouth.

"Sshhhhh. Easy, baby."

The voice was soft and familiar.

Kirsten spun around. "What — *Dad!* You scared me out of my mind!"

"Sorry," her father replied. "But I guess that makes two of us."

Kirsten heard footsteps in the back hall.

"*Ed?*" her mom's voice called from inside. "*Is that you?*"

"Make that three," Dr. Wilkes continued, as the back door swung open.

Kirsten's mom looked washed out. Her face was a tight mask of weariness, her eyes blood-shot and fearful.

"It's okay, Laurie," Dr. Wilkes said. "She's here."

The tension disappeared from her mom's face. At first Kirsten thought she was going to cry.

Then Kirsten was sure her mom was going to kill her.

"Out with *a friend*?" she said. "Until eleven on a weekday?"

"*Eleven*?" Kirsten squeaked. "Is it that late?"

Her mom turned away sharply. Kirsten watched her go straight to the kitchen phone and pound out a number.

Dr. Wilkes held the door open for Kirsten. "I've been out looking for you," he said. "I think we need to have a little family talk."

"Sorry . . ." Kirsten mumbled. The word sounded so limp and false.

Her mom's voice rang out: "Yes, hello, Officer Schweid, it's Laurie Wilkes. We've found her . . . yes, she's fine. . . ."

"She called the *police*?" Kirsten asked.

Dr. Wilkes looked as surprised as Kirsten. He let out a deep breath. "I take it back. A *long* family talk."

Some talk. Kirsten's parents yelled, Nat peeked in now and then for a well-timed giggle, and Kirsten sat playing with the ends of her hair.

At the end she had to go straight to her room, do her homework, and skip David Letterman — who just happened to have Jason Priestley on that night.

Arrgggh.

Tried, convicted, and sentenced. Without any defense.

It was unfair with a capital U.

Well, one good thing came out of it. Kirsten hadn't had to mention Rob. She couldn't have, even if she'd wanted to. Her parents had been too busy hollering at her and each other.

Now, in the quiet of her dark, wood-paneled bedroom, she could finally think. About the strange day.

About Rob.

Kirsten didn't know how to feel. Rob had been such a pig. A liar. A *criminal*, for coaching her without a driver's license. He was the worst, most disgusting stereotype of a teen-age male goon.

But he had been wonderful, too. Kind, patient, funny, sensitive. Not to mention a terrific teacher. Could all of that have been an act?

If so, Rob was a fantastic actor.

And an absolutely rotten person.

Kirsten sighed. Maybe Rob had lost his head. Become swept away beyond his ability to control himself by his ardor for Kirsten. Maybe he was still in the park, grieving over his impulsive mistake.

Right.

Kirsten emptied her backpack onto her desk. She would let him make the next move. If he wanted her, he'd have to try real hard. Prove to her he could be trusted.

If he didn't try at all, too bad. He was history.

But she sure hoped he *did* try.

Kirsten's math notebook was upside down. As she turned it over, a handful of papers slid across the desk.

One of them was her flyer for the driver's ed contest.

She picked it up and looked at the photo of the Escort.

Her heart began to beat faster. She blinked, as if that might change what she was seeing.

The car *was* in profile. Almost completely. It was angled toward Kirsten, but just a bit.

She let go of it and watched it flutter back to her desktop.

What was going on here?

"Mom?"

Kirsten's voice was so parched, she barely heard her own call. She swallowed, but she didn't call out again.

What was she going to tell her mom? *I think the car in this flyer moves. You see, I first noticed something weird about Rob's flyer. . . . Rob? Oh, he's the unlicensed driver who let me drive his car to the park tonight.*

Uh-huh. Sure.

Time for a reality check.

Okay. First of all, Rob's flyer. The position of KIRSTEN'S CAR hadn't changed at all. Rob must have had *two flyers*. He had written the words on one *in advance*, knowing that he was going to charm Kirsten. Then, when he looked for it in the car and couldn't find it, he wrote on another flyer — then unexpectedly pulled out the first at the park!

Perfect explanation, except for one thing.

It sounded stupid.

But hey, Maria had said Rob was a scuzzball. And he had lived up to it in the park, so he wasn't immune from stupid actions.

Kirsten's flyer? Well, if she were a company sponsoring a contest, would she necessarily give each kid an identical photo? No. Maybe each flyer had a different angle of the Escort. Contestants could drool over the different features in each other's photos.

It made sense.

Case closed.

She opened her math book.

But before she started, she stuffed the flyer in her desk drawer.

Of all the nights to have three killer assignments, it would have to be tonight. By the time Kirsten flopped into bed, it was almost 12:30. Nat had been sleeping for an hour and a half. Even the intermittent conversation from her parents' room had stopped.

Kirsten shut her eyes, but her mind was wide open. Unanswered questions poked up, keeping her awake. *Why* had Rob lied to her? Why had he chosen her? What were those strange expressions on his face when she asked simple questions?

And what about Kirsten's driving skills? Without Rob's magic, was she doomed to slide back to Advanced Spaz?

Images began to float around now. Gwen's smug face, Mr. Busk's scowl, Maria's accusing frown, Nat's idiotic trick, the stained letter to the Trangs. . . .

A face began to loom in her mind, uninvited,

translucent. It was an Asian face, vague and ill-formed, obviously an idea of how Nguyen Trang might have looked.

In her agitated half sleep, Kirsten felt for him — separated from his parents, in love with a fickle creep like Gwen, driven to take his own life.

Chances are he had slept in this room, Kirsten thought. It was the second biggest bedroom in the house. The wood paneling made a definite *boy* statement.

Wood paneling . . . had to go . . . wallpaper . . . brighter, cheerful . . .

Kirsten's thoughts were jumbling, streaming into the rhythms of sleep.

"*Ohhhhhh* . . ."

When she heard the moan, her eyes popped open.

The room was black and still. Silent.

A cat, Kirsten assured herself. They sound so much like people when they wail.

She forced her eyes shut. She thought of sheep. Sugar plums. *Boring things*. Math. The business section of the newspaper. Upholstery. Cable TV ads for carpet cleaning . . .

"*Ohhhhhh* . . ."

She was wide awake and flying.

It was from her closet.

No. She had just been in her closet to get her pj's.

Nat! That's who it was.

"Nat?"

No answer.

"N-Nat?"

It had to be a dream.

She had dreamed the noise. It was gone now.

I'm awake, she told herself. *No need to be afraid.*

But something was terribly wrong. Kirsten's skin was prickling. Her breaths came in shallow spasms.

Leave this room, her instincts screamed.

The moon was just over the house, casting pale light through her half-drawn shades. Kirsten's eyes were adjusting, taking in more shadows and shapes.

Then they stopped at the closet door.

It was vibrating.

Kirsten's stomach lurched around inside her like a small, frightened animal. She sat up. Blinked.

The motion stopped. The door was completely still.

Suddenly the living room couch seemed like an excellent bedtime choice. Kirsten quietly pulled back the covers. She swung her feet over the side.

Her legs were shaking as she tiptoed toward the door.

Then she froze.

A shadow was emerging from beneath her closet door, black and growing slowly.

But the door was shut tight.

Kirsten choked on a gasp. She watched the shadow spread toward her. It inched into a small rectangle of moonlight on the floor.

And then she could see that the shadow was not a shadow at all. Nor was it black.

It was a liquid, and it was red.

Blood red.

Chapter 10

Kirsten opened her mouth to scream.

Nothing.

Not a sound.

She tried to move.

Release emergency brake!

She unlocked her knees and bolted.

Kirsten's knuckles smacked the door. She fumbled for the knob and yanked on it.

She hadn't reached the bottom of the stairs before she heard her parents' bedroom door open.

She looked up to see them heading toward her room. *"Mom! Dad! Don't!"*

"Don't what?" answered her mom groggily. "Is . . . is someone in there?"

"No! Not someone!" Kirsten shot back up the stairs and pulled her door shut.

Her dad looked as if she'd lost her mind. "Kirsten, what are you hiding?"

"Nothing! It's just — it's just — "

How can I say it?

Now Nat's door was opening. Rubbing his eyes, he walked out of the room. "Can't you guys be quiet?"

"Kirsten, what is in there?" Mrs. Wilkes demanded, her brow knitted with concern. "Did you see a mouse?"

"Gross," Nat grumbled.

Dr. Wilkes reached for the doorknob. "They never told us there were *rodents* — "

"No, Dad! Don't open it!"

"Kirsten, stop it!" her mother snapped.

"Open it!" Nat squealed. "I want to see!"

Dr. Wilkes let go of the knob and folded his arms. "Quiet, please!" he bellowed.

The stairway landing fell silent.

"I will postpone opening this door until Kirsten informs us what we have to look forward to. Kirsten, the floor is yours."

All eyes stared at her. She took a deep breath and tried to blow out the fear that clogged her body. "Okay. I — I was going to sleep when I saw this blood — I mean, it looked like blood — it was liquid, and it was coming out of the closet — "

"Whoa! Cool!"

Nat zipped past them all and barged into the room.

"*Nooooooooo!*" Kirsten shrieked.

Slam! Nat pulled the door shut behind him.

Before anyone could get to the door after him, it slowly opened again.

Nat appeared. Behind him the room was still dimly moonlit. His eyes were wide, his mouth hung open.

"N-Nat?" Kirsten said. "Are you all right?"

He looked at her obliquely and tried to speak. Then his eyes rolled into his lids and he fell to the floor in a heap.

Kirsten stared in shock.

"*Nat!*" Mrs. Wilkes gasped.

Dr. Wilkes quickly knelt beside him and cradled his head. "Natty? Can you hear me?"

Nat's eyes flickered open. A tiny, growing smile gave way to a spurt of laughter. "*Rank!*"

Kirsten drooped against the wall. It had been twice in two days for his stupid tricks.

Mrs. Wilkes shook her head in disgust.

"Not a smart move, Nathaniel," Dr. Wilkes said. "I don't ever want to see you do that again."

"You know," Mrs. Wilkes seethed, "it's after one o'clock in the morning — "

As her parents lectured Nat, Kirsten took a step into her room.

Shivers seized her. The closet area was pitch-black, out of range of the slanting hallway light.

Girding herself, she flicked on the switch by her door.

Desk. Computer. Bookshelves. Bed. Closet. Carpet. All blinked into her vision.

Kirsten stared at the carpet next to the closet door. She closed her eyes. Shook her head. Opened her eyes again.

What she saw made her skin crawl.

"You feel better now?" her mom said over her shoulder.

Kirsten could not answer.

This was impossible. The carpet was as blue as always. Not a trace of blood.

She walked in slowly, touching the area with her toes. It was bone-dry.

But she had seen it. *After* she had awakened.

"Where was it, honey?" her dad asked.

"Under the closet door," Kirsten replied, her voice a whisper.

Dr. Wilkes went to the door and opened it. Kirsten's clothes hung undisturbed, her shoes lay in an unruly pile on the dry floor.

"It was a bad dream, sweetheart," her mom said, putting her hand on Kirsten's shoulder.

"I guess."

"It's been tough moving from our old house, hasn't it?" Mrs. Wilkes folded Kirsten into a warm embrace.

But not even her mother's arms could warm the icy chill that had formed inside her.

When the traffic light turned green at 8:45 the next morning, at the corner of Burnside and Merrick, Kirsten Wilkes was waiting.

"All right, you know what to do," Mrs. Wilkes said.

Kirsten let her foot slip off the brake and stepped on the gas. Her signal clicked softly, then stopped as she turned.

"Good job! Wow, you really are getting the hang of this!"

Kirsten smiled. *Thanks to Rob Maxson,* she wanted to say. *Who also tried to seduce me last night in the park, by the way, Mom.*

No. She couldn't talk about it. Not yet. Not before she gave Rob his chance. Even he deserved that.

Her mom had gotten very close to bringing Rob into the conversation over that morning's breakfast. Kirsten had managed to veer away from the topic by agreeing to make everybody's pancakes.

She'd also managed to slip a little too much salt in Nat's. Enough to ruin them in retaliation for the night before. He spit them out — and got in trouble.

She felt guilty about that. A little.

By now, she was convinced the pool of blood was a dream. She had slept on the living room couch that night, then double-checked her room in the morning.

Sometimes dreams seemed so real.

As she drove past the park, she noticed flashing lights in the wooded area behind the pond. They distracted her just enough to make her veer into the oncoming lane.

"Hey! Don't kill us!" Mrs. Wilkes said. "The ambulance over there's already taken."

Kirsten snapped back to full attention and pulled smoothly to the front of the school.

Her mom applauded as Kirsten shifted to Park and undid her seat belt. "What an improvement! I'm proud of you."

"Thanks, Mom."

They kissed good-bye, and Kirsten slipped out of the car.

Homeroom was still thirteen minutes away. Slinging her backpack over her shoulder, she walked toward the park.

As she passed the hedgerow that separated the park from the school, she could see the flashing lights clearly. Two police cars were parked at a skewed angle on the grass, along with the ambulance — in the same area she'd been in the night before.

A crowd had formed behind a yellow police tape, strung between trees. Her view of the accident site was blocked by the people, but over their heads she could see the ambulance doors swing open.

Kirsten picked up her pace. Sobs and murmurs floated toward her, growing louder, drowning out the incessantly cheerful birds overhead.

At the edge of the crowd, Kirsten stood on her toes and angled herself to get a view. Paramedics were loading a body on a stretcher into the ambulance. The body was covered by a white sheet from head to toe.

She caught a glimpse of deep tire marks, slashing through the soil. They seemed to come from the pond itself. A trash basket lay flattened near a bench, papers and wrappers strewn beside it.

Kirsten shouldered her way to the front of the crowd, most of whom were stunned schoolmates.

She almost didn't see Maria, weeping in Virgil's arms.

"Hi, Kirsten," Virgil said softly.

"What happened?" Kirsten asked.

Maria lifted her head. Her eyes were red, and mascara ran down her cheeks like witch's fingers. "He — he was — run over," she said between sobbing gulps. "Some kid found him this morning."

"*Who* was run over?" Kirsten's pulse was racing.

Virgil patiently took hold of her wrist and for some reason she wanted to slap him.

In a barely audible voice, he said, "It was Rob, Kirsten."

Chapter 11

"Not funny, Virgil!"

The words leaped from Kirsten's mouth. They protected her. Kept her from believing Virgil's sick joke.

Nat, Rob, Virgil — all of them thought they could walk over her. Scare her brains out. Take advantage. Lie.

But Maria just burst into tears all over again.

And because of that, Kirsten knew. She was fooling herself.

Rob was dead.

She pushed her way to the front of the crowd. The paramedics were angling the stretcher into place. Putting straps across the body.

One of the straps lifted a section of the sheet. A corner of a black leather jacket flapped out.

Kirsten felt her knees give way.

She grabbed on to the nearest person, who didn't seem to notice. Around her, colors drained away to black and white. People were moving in slow motion. Faces loomed in front of her, pasty and distorted.

Then a soft, muffled sound welled up in the back of her mind. It began to grow louder, garbled and human and oh, so indescribably sad. *Ohhhhh . . .* The black and white colors before Kirsten became suffused with red, blood red, pouring from the sky.

The trees were red. The faces around her wept red tears. The clouds moved across the sky like floating bloodclots. *OHHHHH . . .* The moan grew louder and pushed against the inside of her head.

Kirsten felt her eyes crossing. She put her hands to her ears. She pressed against her skull to stop the pressure. To contain the moan before she exploded.

She felt herself buckling, falling to her knees, wanting to scream —

Smack!

The ambulance door slammed shut. Kirsten looked up. Tear-streaked faces were staring down at her. Grief and shock, interrupted by curiosity.

Color had returned. And normal movement.

Between bodies, Kirsten saw a paramedic glance toward her with a tic of concern, then turn away. He joined a coworker, who was comforting a distraught woman in a raincoat and bedroom slippers. Rob's mom, Kirsten realized.

The men and the woman got into the ambulance. With a roar of the engine it drove away, its siren wailing.

Kirsten felt two hands lifting her upward. "Hey, are you all right?" Maria asked.

Am I all right? Sure. I killed Rob, that's all. I left him in the park. Alone. I just up and walked away from him. He didn't think I'd do it. He held his ground. He thought I'd come back to him. He thought he was teaching me a lesson. But I showed him.

Kirsten wanted to throw up.

"Yeah," she croaked. "I'm . . . fine."

Around her, the crying continued, louder. Kids were huddling together to comfort each other, the huddles growing rapidly as more kids arrived.

Out of the corner of her eye, Kirsten spotted a flash of electric purple. A lone figure standing apart from the throng.

At the edge of the park, dressed in a purple

anorak, Gwen Mitchell stood against a stout, peeling sycamore tree. Her eyes stared blankly, calmly, as if she were watching a chess game, but her fingers vigorously worked the locket around her neck.

"Come on, Kirsten, let's go," Maria urged.

Gwen's eyes turned. Now they locked on Kirsten's, and her blank expression changed.

She began walking toward Kirsten, a small, cruel smile growing on her face. Her hand dropped from the locket and reached inside her anorak.

What was she doing?

"Gwen?" Maria whispered.

Kirsten swallowed. Maria and Virgil flanked her on either side.

A dreadful thought shot through Kirsten's mind. Gwen was here last night. She saw. She waited until Kirsten left. Until she could be alone with Rob. And then she . . .

She killed him.

Gwen's hand pulled something from her anorak. Between her fingers it caught the glint of the morning sun.

Where were the police?

"Here." Gwen stood two feet from Kirsten, holding out her right hand. "I think you left these behind."

In her palm was a set of keys. Dangling from it was a small block of wood carved into the name KIRSTEN.

"Where — ?" Kirsten whispered.

"*He* had them," Gwen said, gesturing toward the ambulance. She shrugged. "They won't do him much good now, will they?"

Rob had taken her keys! After she had given him her jacket. *We want your arms to be free.* Another lie. How could she ever have believed him?

What was he planning to do? Sneak into the house at night? She would never know now.

"What are *you* doing with these?" Kirsten grabbed the keys and stuffed them into her own pocket.

Gwen's smile was gloating, triumphant, icy. It cut through Kirsten like a dagger. "I found them. When I found him."

"Gwen, you are sick," Maria said in a choked voice. She tugged Kirsten backward.

But Kirsten could not break herself from Gwen's murderous gaze.

As Gwen took a step forward, her lips drew back from her teeth like a wolf about to pounce. Kirsten felt the hairs rise along the back of her neck.

"I — " Gwen choked on her words. Her

eyes began flashing with emotion, like clouds across the moon. Hatred wrestled with confusion, finally giving way to a wash of sudden tears.

With an anguished cry, Gwen turned on her heels and sprinted away.

"Hey!" Virgil shouted. "That little — " He let go of Kirsten's arm and ran after her.

"Virgil, no!" Maria called after him, but he was lumbering across the sloping, well-trampled lawns, halfway to the sidewalk.

Maria shook her head. "Big hero. He picked today to turn macho. Let's go, Kirsten."

Kirsten let herself be led. She was not aware of walking. Her head seemed swollen and she felt nauseous.

Rob stole my keys. I left Rob alone in the dark. Gwen killed Rob.

Three sentences. Each was like a blow to the stomach.

Maybe Rob had taken the keys accidentally. Maybe he would have given them back today, with a charming apology.

Maybe everything would be just fine.

But Gwen had been in the park. And now the world was turning inside out. Good was bad, dead was alive, hope was fear.

Rob was dead.

"Oh . . ." Kirsten's legs gave way again. She slumped to the ground, taking Maria with her.

A sob exploded from deep within her. Kirsten could hold it back no longer. She wailed with a strangled, anguished fury so loud and strange it seemed to be coming from somewhere else.

"Who-o-oa, sshhhh . . ." Maria said, drawing her closer, massaging her back. The two of them rocked back and forth, sitting on the dewy grass. "It's okay."

Kirsten pushed away. "It's *not* okay, Maria! This is all my fault!"

"Ssshh, what are you talking about?"

"You saw Rob pick me up yesterday. Well, he gave me a driving lesson, and it was — it was phenomenal. I felt so confident, so . . . *cared for*." Kirsten sniffed back her tears. "We went to a movie and dinner, and then — and then we ended up here."

Maria's eyes widened. "*You* came to the park with Rob last night?"

"We didn't — oh, Maria, he tried to — *you* know, and I told him off. Stomped away. Left him here."

"But he was alive . . . right?"

"Of *course* he was alive! You didn't think *I* — "

"No! No, Kirsten. Go on."

"I walked home. That was it. Until now."

Maria looked away and let out a huge sigh.

"What should I do?" Kirsten continued. "Call the police?"

"No. I don't think so."

"But it's my fault, Maria. I was here. I'm the only one who knows that!"

"You didn't kill him," Maria said levelly. "Gwen did. That seems clear to me."

Kirsten looked at the grass. "I . . . I guess."

"You'd be a fool to tell the police you were at the park with Rob. They'll just suspect *you* and not Gwen."

"But *why*, Maria? Why would she do such a thing?"

Maria shook her head. "Gwen's crazy, Kirsten. She's been that way for months."

"*I want to kill her!*" The words escaped Kirsten's mouth before she could stop them. But she had no desire to take them back.

"Shh, don't say that."

"Okay. Does New York have the death penalty?"

"Nope."

"All right, then I want to get her locked up for life." Kirsten picked herself up and looked at the accident scene. One of the police cars was still there. "I *am* going to talk to the police. I'll tell them everything Gwen said."

"Uh, guess again, Kirsten." Maria stood up next to her. "Look, I know you're upset, but think straight. Gwen gave you *your* keys, remember? She said Rob had them. How's that going to look? *You're* the one that has to worry about the police. If Gwen goes to them, you're in trouble."

Kirsten stared at her best friend. Maria's eyes were still teary, but firm as stone. "Kirsten, like it or not, you are Suspect Number One."

Chapter 12

Kirsten felt her whole body go slack. *Suspect Number One*. Great. She'd live the rest of her life unable to tell the truth. Feeling tormented by a murder she didn't commit.

The pounding of footsteps made her and Maria look toward the street. Virgil was approaching them, red-faced and out of breath.

"I lost her," he said. "She can really fly."

The three of them stood there, not knowing what to say next. Kirsten thought of telling Virgil what she'd just explained, but Maria was looking at her with a definite *No* in her eyes.

This was best kept a very *small* secret. For as long as possible.

Until Gwen blabbed it to *The New York Times*.

Schoolmates were shuffling past them now,

arms around each other's shoulders, sniffling, crying, speaking in hushed voices.

"Maybe we should go," Maria suggested.

"Yeah." Virgil put an arm around Maria, and she put hers around Kirsten.

Together they walked toward the school.

The lobby felt like a funeral home. Students who had missed or avoided the park soon found out what had happened. A few ran out the door. Some were weeping. Others clearly wanted to go to the park and see what they'd missed.

A P.A. announcement instructed all students to go to homeroom. Then the classes would proceed to the auditorium for an assembly.

Kirsten and Maria were in different homerooms, but they managed to sit together in the auditorium. The place was practically silent. Like a movie theater immediately after a sad film has ended.

Only this was no movie.

"By now we all know about the tragic accident that took the life of Robert Maxson," began the principal, Mr. Eliades.

Accident? Kirsten suddenly whirled around to look for Gwen. Of course, she was nowhere to be seen.

Kirsten couldn't listen to the rest. Concentration was impossible. She caught a few words as they wafted by her: *precautions, risky behavior, buddy system.* . . .

How to Prevent Future Occurrences. That was the topic of the speech. Did Mr. Eliades care that one of his students was dead? Would he have cared more if it were the class valedictorian, the star football player, instead of Scuzzball Rob?

A cry lodged in Kirsten's throat, and it came out sounding like a hiccup. Maria began rubbing her back.

". . . After dark, do not travel outside alone. . . ." Mr. Eliades droned on.

"He wasn't *alone*," Kirsten whispered.

"Ssshhhh," Maria urged.

Four hours later (well, it *felt* that long), the students were dismissed for the rest of the day.

Kirsten, Virgil, and Maria paused by the entrance. "Gwen wasn't there, was she?" Maria asked.

"No," Kirsten said.

"Are you kidding?" Virgil snorted. "The way she was running, she's halfway to Montauk by now."

"I hope she keeps running," Maria grumbled, "right into the ocean."

"I still can't believe she would do something like that," Kirsten said.

"The girl is out of her mind, like I told you," Maria replied. "Ever since Nguyen died. She kind of snapped."

Virgil was nodding in agreement. "It's true."

"That was when Mr. Good Taste over here stopped drooling over her," Maria said, looking at Virgil.

"Thanks, Maria." Virgil glowered at her.

"I mean, I don't know what he saw in her — "

"Maria, stop. . . ."

"Who knows? It could have been Virgil instead of Rob out there — "

"*Maria!*" Virgil looked disgusted. He turned and stalked away.

Kirsten watched him for a moment. "You can be hard on him, you know — "

When she turned back, Maria was crying.

"Sorry," Maria said. "I just got carried away. I mean, he was so in love with her. He couldn't see how she was using poor Nguyen. He couldn't see *anything*! You see how fast he left us when Gwen ran away?"

"You think he still likes her?"

"I don't know what I think anymore."

Now it was Kirsten's turn to comfort Maria.

"Don't worry. We're all upset by this. Give him a call, talk it over."

"Yeah. Okay, Kirsten. See you."

"Bye."

As Maria headed toward her house, Kirsten walked toward Merrick Road. The police cars were still in the park, but the crowd had dwindled. Curious passersby outnumbered students now.

Kirsten veered into the park. She retraced her steps from the night before. When she reached the police cordon, she stopped. Beyond it, police officers eyed her warily as they sipped coffee and talked to each other.

Kirsten looked at the tire tracks that had gouged through the soil.

Tire tracks.

Cars weren't allowed in the park. Even if someone managed to drive in, the footpaths were narrow, winding, and rutted. The trees had grown so close it would be practically impossible to get from the street to the far side of the park.

But the tracks seemed to come from the pond. Where they began, the flattened trash basket lay forgotten. It was maybe ten feet from where she and Rob had been sitting. The tire tracks continued from there, went toward the bench, and continued a few more feet until they stopped inside the cordon.

Maybe Gwen drove close to the edge of the water and quietly sneaked up on Rob. He got up to run, but it was too late.

But the soil near the pond was soggy. The tires would have left impressions the whole way. Or gotten stuck.

And Rob would have seen it — or heard it.

Kirsten walked closer to the trash basket. It was more than flattened; it looked ripped apart, as if a bomb had exploded inside it.

Among the stuff strewn about, Kirsten recognized one item. A glossy sheet of paper, crumpled and charred, with the words, WIN THE CAR OF YOUR DREAMS! visible.

The flyer she'd thrown at Rob.

Kirsten's breath quickened. It was the last thing they had looked at together. She glanced at the cops. They were deep in conversation. Quietly she knelt down and picked up the flyer.

She read the words KIRSTEN'S CAR written across the top.

But her heart stopped when she looked underneath.

The car in the photo was gone.

Chapter 13

It had to be a trick.

Rob must have had several of these flyers. He was planning to show Kirsten different ones throughout the night. To confuse her. Tease her.

The flyer Kirsten had thrown at Rob had a photo of the Escort. Surely if she snooped around, she'd find it.

Kirsten kicked aside the scattered papers. She looked over the cordon, scanned the ground. She saw the cigarette pack Rob had dropped, but nothing else. Now some people in the crowd were staring at her. And some cops.

Kirsten felt weak again. Knotted. Shivery.

She turned from the crowd, trying to look as normal as possible, and headed home.

Shock. Grief. Betrayal. Fear. One feeling

flooded over the other. The neighborhood seemed to be spinning. Kirsten reached her house in a daze.

When she opened the door, she was hit by the smell.

It was suffocating now, no longer a vague stuffiness. The smell was heavy, rotten, as if a dead animal were decomposing in some hidden corner.

Was. this what it felt like to lose your mind? First you start seeing things, then hearing things, then smelling dead animals in your nice middle-class house. . . .

Next comes the lobotomy.

CALL EXTERMINATOR! Kirsten wrote on a sheet of paper by the kitchen phone.

The smell was making her dizzy. She went to one of the kitchen's casement windows and began cranking it open.

Bleeeeep!

Kirsten jumped at the sudden sound.

The phone. Calm down.

She lifted the receiver. "Hello?"

"Kirsten!" Her mom was practically yelling. "I just heard what happened. Are you all right?"

"Yeah. Fine."

"How did you get home?"

"Walked."

"By yourself?"

"*Mom*, you raised me in New York City, remember? I can walk home alone in Port Lincoln."

I just can't stand this house, that's all. Plus I may soon be wanted for the killing of the boy who kept me out late and stole my keys, who was actually run over by an ex-girlfriend in a car that materialized out of thin air. Now excuse me while I look for a Ford Escort that fell out of a photo.

If she even began telling her parents any of this, forget it. Off to the psychiatric ward.

"Oh, Kirsten," her mom said, "I'm so sorry. What an *awful* thing to happen. Did you know the boy?"

Kirsten bit her lip. "A . . . a little."

"Sweetheart, you sound upset. Do you need me to come home?"

"I'll be all right. Maybe I'll go over to Maria's or something."

"Just be careful." Her mom sighed. "Now you see why your dad and I are so concerned when you stay out late. Don't be fooled. These days, just because it's a suburban neighborhood doesn't mean it's safe."

"I know, Mom. Thanks. See you later."

"Bye-bye."

Silence again.

Where was Nat? Hateful as he was, at least he'd be another body in the house.

Ugh. Bad choice of words.

Kirsten began opening all the windows she could. The wind was raw with a hint of winter, but it swept away the musty air.

And it cleared the cobwebs from Kirsten's mind, which began working like crazy.

Maybe Rob did see Gwen. Maybe he saw her drive up in the car and waited for her. He assumed she'd stop. Then, at the last minute, she sped up and nailed him.

But why would she have stuck around the scene of the crime? And where did she put the car?

It was as if the car had just dropped from the sky.

Appeared out of nowhere.

Suddenly Kirsten bolted from the kitchen. She ran upstairs. Darting across her room, she yanked open her desk drawer.

The flyer was still there. On top of the letter to the Trangs.

She took the flyer out and stared at it.

The Escort was no longer in profile. It was angled toward her.

It had moved.

"Oh my God."

Kirsten slapped the flyer on her desk.

Crazy.

She had put this flyer in the drawer. The car had been in profile. No one had switched it.

Losing my mind.

Rob's Escort had moved, too. Much farther. The last time Kirsten saw it, it had practically been facing front.

No. The *second*-to-last time.

The *last* time, it was gone.

And Rob had been run over.

"No!"

Kirsten's shout died without an echo. From her desktop, the Escort's grille looked like a leering face.

It was waiting.

Waiting to turn full circle.

And then what? Then it would run her over, too?

A laugh exploded from Kirsten. It sounded like a squeal, shrill and unexpected.

This was insane. Absolutely looney tunes. Cars did not jump out of photographs. It was impossible.

For God's sake, throw it out!

Kirsten reached for the flyer. Her eyes caught a glimpse of the letter in her drawer.

Mr. and Mrs. Trang.

She had forgotten about that. She was supposed to forward it.

Then it began.

The moaning.

It wasn't exactly a sound. Kirsten wasn't hearing it through her ears. It was vibrating in her bones, careening up her body to her brain, where it gathered force until she thought she would split in two.

"Ohhhhh . . ."

"Ohhhhh . . ."

Was this what happened before Rob was killed?

Kirsten had to throw the flyer out. Her fingers closed around it but it was like touching a hot coil.

"Yeeow!"

She put her throbbing fingers in her mouth. They were on fire.

Fire.

Paper caught fire. Paper could not be as hot as that.

But the flyer looked completely normal. Not even a wisp of smoke. And Kirsten felt her eyes drawn again to the letter in her still-open drawer.

Mr. and Mrs. Trang.

Forget the flyer. *Mail the letter. Mail it now.*

The urge was pounding through her. She grabbed a red marker and completed what she'd written already, until it read: ADDRESSEE MOVED. PLEASE FORWARD.

And then she knew. Somehow she knew who was invading her. Forcing her attention away from the flyer. Making her mail this letter.

"Nguyen?" The word escaped her mouth in a parched whisper.

She looked at her closet.

And then, like the sudden end of a wrenching nightmare, the moaning stopped.

Chapter 14

"Nguyen?" she repeated.

The letter shook in her hand as she stepped toward her closet. That was where the moaning had first come from. And the blood.

She reached toward the doorknob. Fear clamped her like a vise. Her fingers stopped inches away.

Balling her hand into a fist, she knocked.

"Nguyen? Uh, anybody there?"

She waited, then knocked again.

Slowly she wrapped her fingertips around the knob.

Knock-knock-knock-knock!

Kirsten jumped back from the door and screamed at the top of her lungs.

She fell to the floor and caught her breath. It was the front door.

The knocking had come from downstairs. Calm down.

Knock-knock-knock-knock!

Kirsten ran to her window and looked outside. An unfamiliar bike was propped up against a maple tree out front.

She ran downstairs and through the house, then pulled open the front door.

"Doesn't your bell work?" Virgil was pressing the button repeatedly.

"No," Kirsten replied. "It's busted."

Virgil looked over Kirsten's shoulder into the house. "Hey, nice place."

"Thanks."

"I was never in here before."

"No?"

"I didn't know Nguyen."

"Want to meet him?"

"Huh?"

"Nothing."

Virgil looked at her oddly. "Is something wrong, Kirsten? You look like you saw a ghost."

"No!" Kirsten shot back. *Just heard one, that's all.*

Virgil shrugged. "Sorry. Didn't mean to be critical. I, uh, just wanted to apologize to you.

You know, for walking away after school like that. When Maria and I had that argument."

"Why are you apologizing to *me*?"

"It was . . . you know, rude of me to just storm away without saying good-bye or anything."

"That's okay. I mean, we're all . . . tense."

Kirsten had no idea Virgil was so polite. The apology seemed a little ridiculous. But boy, was she glad for the company.

"Uh, can I come in?" Virgil asked with an awkward smile.

"Oh, sorry! Sure . . . sure."

Virgil stepped in and plopped himself on the living room sofa.

Sniff, sniff. He scrunched his nose. "Do you smell something funny?"

Kirsten winced. "We, uh, we're not sure what that is."

"I can't get over what happened," Virgil said, shaking his head. "I mean, *Rob* — I knew him."

Kirsten sat opposite him on a chair. "Me, too."

"You never think it'll happen to someone you know, and then — you know?"

"Yeah. I know. . . ." They both shook their heads sadly and looked around. Kirsten felt tongue-tied. Virgil was a nice guy, but she still didn't know him well. "Um, where's Maria?"

"Her dad took the day off," Virgil replied with a sigh, "so the whole family could talk about Rob's death with a shrink. I didn't want to stay home alone."

"Oh." A shrink. What a good idea. Leave it to the Siroccos.

"Can I have something to drink?"

"Of course. Sorry! Orange juice okay?"

"Perfect. I'll come with you. See your house."

"Okay." Kirsten led him out of the living room, saying, "This is the dining room . . . the kitchen . . ."

Kirsten smiled as Virgil pretended to be impressed. Poor Virgil. Too afraid to be alone, without his girlfriend. It was kind of sweet that he came over.

Kirsten was feeling a little less tense as she got some orange juice from the fridge and poured two glasses. Virgil was a good guy. Intelligent. He seemed trustworthy.

"Yum," he said. "I haven't had anything to drink all day."

Kirsten took a long gulp. "Virgil, you think Gwen really did it?"

Virgil furrowed his brow. "Well, she kind of admitted it."

"But you *know* her, right? I mean, she is obnoxious, but she doesn't seem like a murderer."

"Jeffrey Dahmer didn't seem like a murderer, either. What are you getting at, Kirsten? Do you have any other ideas?"

Kirsten swallowed. She was dying to tell someone what she'd seen.

"Well, there's been some really strange stuff going down lately," Kirsten began.

"Like?"

Go for it, Kirsten said to herself.

"Virgil, do you happen to have that contest flyer we got in driver's ed?"

"Maybe." Virgil began emptying his pockets — candy wrappers, coins, a bankcard, pieces of tissue, rubber bands, paper clips. . . . "Wait a minute."

He ran into the living room and came back with his coat, rummaging through the pockets. "Here it is."

Virgil held out a folded piece of paper and Kirsten grabbed it.

She quickly opened it and laid it out on the table.

His Escort was angled forward, all right.

Even more than hers had been. Almost as far as Rob's.

"There!" she exclaimed. "Do you remember what this looked like when you first got it?"

Virgil looked at it quizzically. "Flatter. Cleaner."

"Come upstairs — and don't get any ideas."

"*Kir*sten . . ."

Both of them tromped up the stairs to Kirsten's room. She pointed to the flyer on her desk. "Look at that."

Virgil seemed ill at ease. He looked around the room nervously. "Was this Nguyen's room?" he asked.

"I don't know," Kirsten replied. "Why?"

"Just curious." He peered at the flyer. "Yeah . . . so? Hey, wait. The picture's different."

"*Hallelujah!* You see? It's moving!"

Virgil threw back his head and laughed. "Kirsten, you are weird. They must have printed different versions."

"That's what I thought, too. But — "

But Rob's "version" jumped off the page. That was where this conversation was leading. And Kirsten couldn't tell him that. She hadn't even told Maria.

"But what? What does this have to do with Gwen?"

"Nothing. I . . . guess I'm just jumpy."

Virgil looked at her as if she'd just pulled a bicycle out of her nose. "Right. Uh . . . can I use your bathroom?"

"Yeah. Go through my mom and dad's room, and it's the door next to the attic."

Virgil disappeared, and Kirsten went downstairs. She felt like a fool. She should never have mentioned anything to Virgil.

In the kitchen she began assembling ingredients for a bagel and cream cheese. She took out an extra one in case Virgil was hungry.

She made her own, toasting the bagel, slathering it with cream cheese, and stuffing it with lettuce and sliced tomatoes. She read the newspaper as she ate.

Virgil was still upstairs as she finished.

She put her dish in the dishwasher. Where was he?

Nat would do the same thing. Disappear into the bathroom and emerge ages later, having read an entire Hardy Boys novel.

But Virgil hadn't brought anything in with him.

He was taking an awfully long time.

She thought about going upstairs, but decided against it. Instead she began preparing the second bagel.

Whoooooooo . . .

A wind was whipping up outside. Kirsten gazed out the window.

Odd. The sun was shining brightly. Not a leaf was moving.

Kirsten shrugged and slit the bagel in half.

Whhacckkk!

The door to the back foyer opened and smacked against the wall.

With a thundering crash, the china plate on the wall fell to the floor and broke into a thousand pieces.

Chapter 15

Thump thump thump thump thump thump . . .

"Kirsten?"

Virgil appeared at the bottom of the stairs. He stared at the shards of the ceramic plate. "What happened?"

"I don't know." Kirsten's right hand ached. She looked down and realized she'd been clutching the bread knife tightly, as if she were about to be attacked. She set it down on the table. "I was making a bagel and cream cheese when the door flew open."

"Whoa. Must be some wind."

They both looked through the opening and into the foyer. Just beyond it was the back door. Tightly shut.

"Was that open?" Virgil asked.

"No."

Virgil gave her a perplexed look. "Then where . . . ?" His voice trailed off.

"See, Virgil, I told you some strange stuff was happening."

"Dwee-dee-dee-doo, dwee-dee-dee-doo . . ." Virgil began singing the theme to *The Twilight Zone.*

"Not funny. Help me clean up. My mom is going to kill me. This was valuable."

"Couldn't be too valuable if you can't eat off it," Virgil groused as Kirsten handed him a dustpan.

They swept up the mess and dumped it in the trash.

"Thanks," Kirsten said as she put away the broom and pan. "Are you hungry?"

"No, thanks," Virgil replied. "I should be going."

Kirsten walked him to the living room, where he put on his coat. At the door, he turned to Kirsten with a smile. "Listen, I know how you must feel. Gwen won't get away with this."

"If she did it," Kirsten said.

Virgil exhaled loudly. "Kirsten, don't get me wrong, but you're naive. You don't know Gwen — "

"I'm not naive!" Kirsten blurted out. "The tire tracks began in the middle of nowhere! They started near the pond, but they don't trace back along the pond to the street."

Virgil chuckled. "Gwen is a very good driver. Her parents started letting her practice when she was twelve."

"*Twelve?* Isn't that illegal?"

"So's murder. Look, when Gwen sets her mind to something, nothing stops her. That stuff about the tire tracks doesn't surprise me one bit. Piece of cake for a good driver."

"Unlike me, right?"

Virgil looked at the floor. "I — I'm sorry. I didn't mean it that way. And I guess I should have an open mind about Gwen. Innocent until proven guilty, right?"

"Yeah."

"Well, look, if you need me . . ." Virgil smiled. "I'm here for you."

Kirsten felt his hand closing around hers. She felt a surge of warmth for him. "Thanks, Virgil."

His hand lingered a moment. "See you," he said softly. "Soon, I hope."

As he walked to his bike, Kirsten's hand tingled.

And she suddenly felt creepy.

Was it possible? Was Virgil trying to *flirt* with her?

Couldn't be. Not with a friend of his girlfriend. Guys like Virgil weren't that low.

Kirsten walked back through the house. The smell was almost indistinguishable now, flushed out by the chilly air.

She examined the kitchen door, swinging it back and forth a few times. Seemed perfectly normal.

Stepping into the foyer, she checked the back door. It was locked. Opposite that door and next to the kitchen was the basement door.

That one was open.

She peered downstairs, into the darkness.

"Nguyen?"

She flicked on the light and took a step down. Two.

"Anybody there?"

Three. Four.

"Hello?"

At the bottom she stopped and looked around.

What a mess. Moving boxes, old bikes, unneeded furniture — all were strewn about haphazardly.

Kirsten walked back upstairs and turned off

the light. She had to pull the door especially hard to get the latch to click.

Aha! That's what had happened — the door hadn't been shut all the way. It swung open suddenly, making a backdraft that opened the kitchen door.

Kirsten picked the knife up off the table. She went to the counter and finished making the bagel Virgil didn't want.

If in doubt, eat.

As she munched away, she began feeling calmer. It was strange living in a house. Apartment living had been so much simpler — everything on one level, scrunched together. She'd had her whole life to get used to the corners and closets of their old place — which hadn't been hard to do in an Upper West Side "Classic Six." Bedroom, bedroom, bathroom, kitchen, living room, "maid's room." It was small, cozy.

Now she was living in a cavern. Cold and unfamiliar. The house still seemed so *foreign*, as if she were a visitor. No wonder she was hearing things, imagining ghosts. It was probably normal to go through this stage.

Give yourself a break, Kirsten, she thought. *Stop getting all worked up over nothing.*

The blood was a dream, the moaning a migraine headache *(after all, Dad said those were provoked by high stress)*. The flyers — well, there had to be some explanation for those. Gwen had killed Rob. Plain and simple.

And that made her angry.

Where was Gwen now? Halfway across the country, probably, with dyed hair, a new wardrobe, and a fake name.

No one would ever find out how Rob died.

Kirsten got up from the table. If she had to stay silent about the killing to the public, at least she could face the murderer.

If Gwen was home, Kirsten was going to confront her.

She raced upstairs, looked up Gwen's address in the phone book in her parents' room, and wrote it down:

147 Padanarum.

On her way out, she caught a glimpse of an open door to her left.

The attic door.

Had *that* been open before? She didn't think so.

Virgil probably had gotten lost on the way to the bathroom. She closed the door and ran downstairs.

She checked a map of Port Lincoln, which her dad kept by the phone. Padanarum Avenue was across town, near the road to Fenimore Village. She mapped out a route in her mind, bolted outside, and grabbed her bike.

The Port Lincoln streets were quiet; the other schools were in session. Kirsten raced past the new shopping center, where she spotted a bunch of high-school kids hanging out, gathered around a gleaming turquoise Camaro.

Then came the older part of town — big houses, winding streets — and Port Lincoln Park, a rectangular green with crisscrossing pathways and huge maple trees.

Padanarum was one of the streets that began opposite the long side of the park. She sped across the green, taking a middle path, pumping hard, training her eyes on the street signs.

A thick tree partially obliterated one of the signs. She pedaled past the tree, jumped the curb, and landed in the street.

HONNNNNNK!

A red Jeep, hidden by the tree, seemed to come out of nowhere.

Kirsten lost her balance. Her bike went flying.

She tumbled to the street, the screech of brakes in her ears.

Chapter 16

Kirsten hit the blacktop hard. On her back. She felt the heat of the engine. She could see the pebbles wedged in the tire treads, which were sliding, sliding toward her face.

She rolled to the right, gritted her teeth, and closed her eyes.

The impact was more like a yank backward. She felt a sharp pain in her scalp.

The screeching stopped.

Kirsten opened her eyes. A lock of her hair was on the street below her, lying across a black skid mark.

Inches away was the right front tire of the red Jeep.

Kirsten sat up. She was dizzy. She scanned as much of herself as she could. Her khaki pants were ripped at the knee, her elbow was bloody, and the palm of her left hand had a wicked cut.

Plus she was now a little balder.

"You're worse on a bike than in a car!"

Kirsten spun around. The voice was unmistakable.

"Mr. Busk!" she exclaimed, scrambling to her feet. "I'm sorry!"

"Sorry?" Mr. Busk's face was beet red. His eyes bulged with anger. *"Sorry?* You almost gave me a heart attack! You ought to be glad you're alive!"

"I know . . . I *am!"*

"You think you don't have to look both ways on a bike? You think you can just cross wherever you want? *And you want to get your driver's license?"*

He was practically spitting his words. The sickly sweet smell of alcohol blew past Kirsten in putrid gusts. She thought of asking him for some — to put on her cut — but that didn't seem like a wise move.

Besides, he was not going to give Kirsten a chance to speak. After his tirade he turned and stomped back to his Jeep.

With a squeal of tires, he tore off.

The jerk.

The drunken, irresponsible, ought-to-be-fired-if-I-had-the-guts-to-report-him jerk!

Nearly killed me, and he didn't even ask if I was all right!

Besides, couldn't he see her riding across the park? Or would he have, if he were sober?

He was the last person who should be teaching driver's ed, and she vowed to report him to the school officials.

Kirsten stretched her legs and arms. Everything seemed to be intact. She was lucky.

Her bike was even luckier. It had rolled to the curb and fallen onto a soft patch of grass.

A few yards away, in the green, Kirsten spotted an old cement water fountain. She went over and let the water rinse her elbow and palm.

Next she found a bandanna in her jacket pocket and pulled it out. The skin that had scraped off her palm hung in a loose semicircular flap. She flipped it over to cover the scrape, then wrapped the bandanna around her hand to hold the skin in place and stop the bleeding.

That would protect it until she got home. The elbow would just have to air out.

Carefully she picked up her bike and started

riding. Padanarum was the street to her left. She turned onto it and looked for number 147.

Kirsten had figured that Gwen's family must have been on the rich side. But that wasn't likely in this neighborhood. The houses were old, small, and close together. Some were neatly kept, but others were run-down, with scraggly, weed-strewn dirt patches for lawns.

Number 147 was on a corner, a modest aluminum-sided colonial-style house with a screened-in porch.

Kirsten slowed down. She could hear the tick-tick-ticking of another ten-speed bike.

A moment later, Gwen shot out of the driveway on the other side of the house, wearing a bulky backpack. Pedaling fast, she headed away from Kirsten.

When Gwen was a block and a half away, Kirsten began to follow.

It wasn't easy keeping Gwen in sight. She darted left and right, taking a winding route through streets Kirsten had never seen before.

At a five-way street corner, Kirsten stopped. Gwen was nowhere in sight.

Poof. End of search.

Kirsten muttered a curse. All that effort — a brush with death — and all Kirsten had to show was a sore back and a souvenir of the Port Lincoln Highway Department embedded in her skin.

Now what? Go back to Gwen's and wait, or go home?

Kirsten looked at the street signs: MAIN ST, BECKWITH AVE, TEICHNER PL. She might as well have been in Bulgaria. Not one name rang a bell.

With a sigh, she headed down Main. It didn't *seem* very main, but you never knew. Sooner or later, something might look familiar.

After a few blocks, Main Street widened. When it intersected with Merrick Road, Kirsten finally had her bearings. A left turn would take her home.

Across Merrick, Main Street looked like an abandoned movie set, a center of town for some mythical village from the 1960s. Among the dilapidated storefronts were a few struggling shops among boarded-up buildings. On one of the lampposts a faded sign proclaimed PORT LINCOLN — BABE RUTH LEAGUE CHAMPS 1971.

Below the sign, Gwen's bike was chained to the post.

Kirsten walked her bike across Merrick. She could see Gwen's back through a shop window with the words, SOMETHING OLD, SOMETHING NEW, printed across in cracking gold letters.

Directly across the street, Kirsten saw an alleyway between two buildings. She ducked into it and kept still.

After a few moments Gwen emerged, putting on her backpack. She looked up and down the street warily.

Gingerly Kirsten backed farther into the alley, out of Gwen's sight.

She counted to fifty and edged forward. Gwen and her bike were gone.

Kirsten stepped out of the alleyway and looked up and down the street. No Gwen.

She looked at the shop again. In its window was a bizarre collection of things: a saxophone, an old manual typewriter, a pair of ice skates, several cameras, a bulky metal computer, and some jewelry on a felt-covered shelf. The dominant color was light brown, as if the display hadn't been dusted since the Babe Ruth championship.

Under the store's logo, smaller letters spelled out, LOANS MADE.

Kirsten had seen plenty of pawnshops in the Big Apple. A person could get an instant loan by giving the shop a valuable item. If the person didn't return after a certain time, the shop could sell the item to the public.

Gwen was putting on her pack as she left. Which meant she had removed it inside.

Had she bought something or left it?

Only one way to find out.

Kirsten chained her bike to the street lamp and walked to the door. Above the door's brass handle was a handwritten sign that said, PLEASE BUZZ.

In the handle was a rolled-up sheet of yellow paper.

Kirsten pulled the sheet out and opened it. A note had been scribbled inside:

Hi, Kirsten!

No, I haven't gone to the police yet, but don't worry, I will.

By the way, Kirsten. How did your parents' car get that dent in the front bumper?

I'll visit you in prison.

Love, Gwen

Chapter 17

The witch! The sneaky, lying, evil, murdering witch!

Gwen was trying to frame her.

The dent in Dad's car looked as if it could have been made by a person. Would the police fall for it?

They might.

But not if they had something else to fall for.

Kirsten folded up the note and stuffed it in her pocket. Gwen meant business, but so did she.

Gwen had gone into this pawnshop for a reason. Why did she need cash? Or did she need to get rid of something?

Kirsten pushed the buzzer. When she heard a buzz back, she pushed on the metal door. It gave way with a loud click.

Her footsteps creaked on the shop's wooden floor. In a dark corner, an old man with a feather duster glanced up briefly, grunted hello, then turned back to his work.

To his left was a human skeleton hanging under a sign that read, BEEN WAITING HERE LONG?

Gee, this place is a barrel of laughs.

A narrow pathway led her between old tables crammed with knickknacks. The air, what was left of it, had a sweet, pungent smell of mildew and aging wood. The front section of the shop had electronic equipment, appliances, and antiques. Racks of old books, records, and cassettes rested against walls covered with ornately framed mirrors and paintings. A ceiling fan whirred noisily above, encrusted with dust and grime.

"Quite a scrape you got," said a voice to her right.

Kirsten turned to see a pudgy, middle-aged man behind the counter. He had a patient, slightly fake smile. On top of his pasty face was a thick crop of waxy black hair. Kirsten wondered how much money he had given a customer for *that*. Probably not a whole lot.

He was leaning back in a chair, reading a dog-eared copy of a horror novel. On the glass counter in front of him was an old-fashioned cash register and a small pile of new-looking clothing and jewelry.

"Yeah, I fell off my bike." Kirsten fingered Gwen's pile. "Hm, this stuff looks nice."

The man's smile widened. "It was just brought in. By a young lady probably about your size. I haven't priced any of it yet, but if you're interested in an item, we can work something out."

Kirsten sifted through the pile — a gorgeous linen shirt, a hideous orange bathing suit, a cheap purse, and a few T-shirts and trinkets.

A small gold ring fell out of a folded skirt. It was set with a diamond-shaped pale purple stone. Kirsten held it up to the light.

The inscription *GM & RM* was engraved inside the band.

Gwen Mitchell and Rob Maxson. This must be stuff Rob gave her.

Stuff Gwen wanted to forget? Evidence?

Her eye fixed on one item among the jewelry.

A locket.

She'd seen that before. Gwen's nervous fingers had been fiddling with it for weeks.

As Kirsten picked the locket off the counter,

she glanced at a stack of business cards in a Lucite holder. She read the top one:

SOMETHING OLD, SOMETHING NEW
Your castaway is another person's treasure.
Loans made * Antiques bought and sold *
Jewelry * Electronics * Clothing
62 Main Street
Port Lincoln, New York 11500
Erik and Olaf Maartens

Olaf.
Why did that name ring a bell?
"Are you Olaf?" she asked the man behind the counter.
"Nope. My father is." He nodded toward the old man.
Oblivious, the old man shuffled around the shop, carrying on a spirited little conversation with no one in particular.
"The car belonged to this little old guy — you know, Olaf, who walks around town talking to himself?"
Maria's words came back to her.
"Wasn't your dad the guy whose car was stolen?" Kirsten asked softly.
The son — Erik — chuckled. "Hey, Pop," he called to the old man, "this girl wants to

know if you were the one whose car was stolen."

Kirsten was mortified. "I didn't mean to — "

"That's okay. He loves to talk about it," Erik said with a wink. "Turned him into an overnight celebrity at age eighty-seven."

Olaf was peering at Kirsten through one eye. The other seemed to be not functioning, half hidden under a droopy lid. As he hobbled over to the counter, Kirsten noticed a faint, stale smell of Old Spice.

"Fifteen years old, that car was," he announced. "I had no theft insurance. Didn't make sense on a wreck like that. Thieves know that. Most of 'em have the decency to take newer cars." He shook his head crankily. "Was a Toyota. Guess the boy liked his country's own products. . . ."

"But Toyotas are from Japan," Kirsten said.

Olaf glared at her, as if she weren't supposed to speak. "Okay, maybe the kid was born in the States, but you know what I mean."

"Well, he was Vietnamese," Kirsten pressed.

Olaf waved a bony hand dismissively. "Yeah. Well, Vietnamese, Japanese, who the hell can tell the difference? 'Specially at night. Anyway, he was wearing a leather jacket, black one, just like them kamikaze pilots in Double-ya Double-ya Two. *They* were Japanese. Also, the kid chose April 18, same day Doolittle bombed Tokyo — same day Yamamoto was killed, too. Now ain't that a pretty little coincidence — "

"It was nighttime, Mr. Maartens?" Kirsten interrupted.

"You bet. I was watching the Mets. Gooden was pitching — "

"And you saw him through a window?"

"Yep."

"And you still got a good look at his face?"

"They found the little rat in my car, didn't they?"

Olaf scrunched up his one good eye at Kirsten — if "good" could be used to describe the glazed, yellowish thing. "I know, you're one of them liberals. Let 'em all in this country, *that's* what you think. Well, see what happened? They think they can get something for nothing! We should force 'em back to their own country — "

"Pop!" Erik said sharply.

The old man sneered, revealing a few worn, yellow teeth separated by gaps you could stick a cigar through. He turned away and went back to his work, muttering further political commentary.

"Sorry," Erik said. "He's not . . . firing all thrusters. Now, if you want to buy something, Miss — "

"No, thanks," Kirsten replied. "Maybe some other time."

She hightailed it outside and unlocked her bike.

As she pedaled home, the houses of Merrick Road sped by in a blur.

He said he saw Nguyen steal his car. An old codger with half an eye, looking through a window at nighttime. It's impressive he was even able to make out a leather jacket!

But the town believed him.

And they didn't believe the Trangs.

Kirsten felt a surge of anger. Had anyone *really* looked into this? Nguyen Trang died without knowing his parents. His aunt and uncle moved away without finding the truth. And no one cared!

What if someone else stole that car? What if someone *was* in the Toyota with Nguyen that night?

When Kirsten got back home, Nat was playing basketball in the backyard. "You made me miss!" was his greeting as she pulled into the driveway.

"Just stuff it, Nat."

"I'm not tall enough! Get it?"

Kirsten ran inside to the sound of Nat's barf-inducing laughter.

She cleaned up her scrapes and cuts in the bathroom and bandaged them securely. Then she called her dad at South Oaks Community Hospital.

"Hi, honey, what's up?" he asked.

"Dad, when people come into the Emergency Room, they all have to sign in, right?"

"Sure."

"Can you get a copy of one of the sign-in sheets — like from April 18?"

"I can try. Why?"

"A . . . demographics project, to demonstrate statistical randomness in community institutions."

Where did *that* come from? Kirsten beamed with pride.

"Sounds serious," her dad said with a chuckle. "I'll get it for you."

"Thanks, Dad!"

Kirsten breathed a huge sigh as she hung up. If another kid was with Nguyen, he couldn't have escaped an accident like that without some serious injury — unless he got out and *pushed* the car over the cliff, which didn't seem too likely.

And South Oaks Community was the only hospital around for miles.

Tip-tip-tip-tip . . . *"Yes!"*

Tip-tip-tip-tip . . . *"Yes!"*

Tip-tip-tip-tip . . . *Bonk. "Foul!"*

Nat's sound effects were beginning to drive Kirsten crazy.

She decided to go upstairs and write in her journal. She hadn't done that since all the weird stuff started happening.

Maybe if she got it all down, she'd be able to figure things out.

She booted her computer and called up her journal. The last date she'd worked on it was September 22, and now it was already mid-October.

She went to the end, then scrolled up to read her last page.

She stared at the orange, glowing screen, her mouth slowly opening in horror:

> *Kirsten, beware!*
> *I know where you live. I know where you sleep. You may think you are safe, but that is part of the plan.*

When you least expect it, you will say good-bye to the world. And you will be unprepared.

Kirsten Wilkes, you can ignore the blood on the floor. But you cannot escape the blood to come.

Your own.

Chapter 18

Kirsten's fingers felt like icicles. Her eyes were magnetized to the screen. The letters seemed to fade and swirl.

She shook her head. She blinked. She prayed she had misread the words. They were a hallucination. Her fall from the bike had given her a concussion, and she was seeing things.

You cannot escape the blood to come. . . .

Kirsten quickly scrolled down. The message continued:

> *And after the blood, Kirsten, comes worse.*
> *Much worse.*
> *Look tonight for the Seeping*
> *Mucus below your windows. To be*

*followed by the Cascade of Puke
from the shower head. Then the
Cake of Fused Boogers in your soap
dish. Of course, if you're quick, you
can feed that to the squiggling little
rodent beckoning you from the toilet
bowl. . . .
NYAH HA HA HA HA HA!!!!!!!!
P.S. You are the worst driver
who ever lived!*

Kirsten heard a squeak outside her door. It became a giggle, then a full-fledged laugh.

"Nat, you rotten, stinking, little slime bucket!" Kirsten screamed, springing from her chair. She flew across the room and threw open the door in time to see her brother jumping the last four steps to the first floor.

She bounded down the stairs and chased him into the street.

Nat sprinted away, howling with laughter. In seconds he had gained most of a block on her.

"I HATE you!" Kirsten shrieked after him.

Cursing under her breath, she stomped back to the house.

She was livid. Nat had gone into her room, turned on her computer, snooped around in her files, found her personal diary, and sabotaged it.

Probably read the whole thing, too!

She went straight to her room and deleted everything he'd written. She stewed for a few minutes, but forced herself to put aside her rage. It was time to write.

She let her fingers fly over the keyboard. She wrote about everything, sometimes not even stopping to put in periods. The date with Rob. Rob's death. Gwen's behavior. The mysterious flyer. The blood. The kitchen door. The doubts she was starting to have about Nguyen Trang's death.

She wrote a lot about Nguyen. Funny how much she was beginning to care about a guy she'd never met. Never *would* meet.

But somehow she felt connected to him. Maybe it was the bedroom (it *had* to have been his; she was sure of it). Maybe it was the unfairness of it all, the assumption that he stole the car and caused his own death.

Kirsten didn't believe it for a minute.

What *did* happen on the night of April 18?

Nguyen didn't know many people. But he did know Gwen. He had to know Rob, too — or *of* him. After all, Rob had been going out with Gwen while Nguyen was pining over her.

What else?

Gwen wanted Rob. Nguyen wanted Gwen (and so did Virgil). Gwen went out with Nguyen, with the cockeyed idea that Rob would get jealous. It was like a soap opera.

And it ended in a death, maybe a murder. But who would have a motive to kill a harmless guy like Nguyen?

Rob? No way. He had dumped Gwen. What did he care who she went out with?

Virgil? Maybe, since Nguyen was going out with the girl he had the hots for. But Virgil was the last person in the world who would murder anyone.

Okay, Kirsten thought. *So I'm Nguyen. What am I thinking about the night I'm about to die? What am I worried about?*

Kirsten recalled something Maria had told her: *"The Trangs kept saying they would find Nguyen's diary, and that would give all the clues to what really happened."*

She opened a new file, and at the top of the first page she typed:

THE DIARY OF NGUYEN TRANG

Off the top of her head, she began composing:

> *I give Gwen so many presents. She
> is so beautiful. Does she really like
> me? I wish she did, but she still
> likes Rob. Maybe I should talk to
> Rob in shop tomorrow. Maybe he
> needs to have a real breakup, in-
> stead of just ignoring her. . . .*

This was ridiculous. How could she put
words in the mouth of someone she didn't
know? Who did she think she was, Nancy
Drew?

She closed the file without saving it. She
was about to shut down the computer when
she thought about Nat.

No way was she going to let him see what
she'd written in her journal.

She took her software manual off the shelf
and found a chapter entitled, "Passwords: Protect Your Sensitive Data."

But her eyes crossed when she began reading. It was too complicated, and she *hated* fig-
uring out computer gobbledegook. She'd get
Maria to help her someday.

For now, she copied her journal file to a
floppy disk, then erased the copy that was on

her hard disk. If Nat tried to snoop around, he'd find nothing.

Slipping the floppy in its paper sleeve, she looked around the room for a place to hide it.

The bookshelves would be the first place Nat would check. The closet was out. Too messy. The disk might get thrown around, bent up. And wedging it between her clothes in her drawers was also a little risky for something so fragile.

Kirsten walked around, idly spinning the disk in her hand.

She noticed the wood paneling was laid on the wall in large sheets. Wherever the sheets met was a seam, floor to ceiling. Along the seam, small nails attached the paneling to the support underneath.

Just above the floor, near her door, one of the seams had warped. A nail or two seemed to be missing, and the sheet of paneling on the left had bowed outward a bit, making a gap.

Kirsten stuck her fingers in the gap and pulled. The wooden sheet had some give, and she could see the wall underneath.

Nat would never think to look there.

Smiling, Kirsten pulled the paneling as far as she could and carefully set the disk inside.

But a disk was already there.

Wrapped in a small plastic bag.

Kirsten pulled it out, sending wisps of dust to the carpet.

She wiped off the dust that obscured the disk label and read the words N. TRANG underneath.

Chapter 19

Kirsten pulled the disk out of the plastic bag. She ran to her computer, inserted it, and typed out the DOS command DIR A:, to get a list of files.

The hard drive popped onto the screen: DATA ERROR READING DRIVE A:.

Terrific. Data error. What on earth did that mean?

She dashed into her parents' room and tapped out Maria's number on the phone.

"Hello?"

"Maria! What's a data error?"

"Uh, excuse me? Come again?"

"It's me — Kirsten! I found a floppy disk that might have Nguyen Trang's diary, but my computer says 'data error.' What does that mean?"

"Could mean the disk is damaged. Could

mean it's not compatible with your system. What kind of computer do you have?"

"Um . . . you know. It sits on a desk and has a screen and big metal thing — "

"*Kirsten* — IBM-compatible or Apple?"

"Well, neither. . . ."

"Oh, *duh*. Didn't they teach you anything in New York City? Does your computer use DOS, Windows, or — "

"DOS!" Kirsten blurted.

"Thank you, Wilma Flintstone. Welcome to the twentieth century. You have an IBM-compatible. Maybe Nguyen's disk is formatted for an Apple."

"Do you have an Apple?"

"Uh-uh — but Virgil has a Mac."

"Thanks! You are the greatest, Maria! See you!"

"Wait, Kirsten. I was about to call you. Tomorrow's the funeral service for Rob. In the morning. Anyone who goes is excused from classes until lunch. Want to go with me?"

Kirsten's smile disappeared. Sadness flowed back into her. "Of course I do. Where should I meet you?"

"My house. It's on the way."

"Okay. See you."

"Bye."

Kirsten tried to shake the funeral out of her mind. She'd have plenty of time for tears tomorrow.

Quickly she called Virgil.

"Virgil, hi, it's Kirsten. I need a Mac."

"Don't we all. I'll meet you there in fifteen minutes."

"What?"

"I could try to make it twelve, but — "

"Meet me where?"

"At Mickey D's."

"No! No! That kind of Mac. Your *computer*!"

"Oh! Hey, well, that's a disk of a different color. I thought you were asking me on a cheap date."

"Virgil, you're a goon."

"Flattery will get you everywhere. Come on over."

Kirsten hung up, grabbed the disk, and ran downstairs. As she sped out the front door, she nearly ran into her mother.

"Hi, Mom! I'll be back in an hour or so!"

"Oh, no, you won't, Kirsten Wilkes! You stop right there!"

Kirsten felt as though someone had thrown a warm blanket of mud over her. "It's okay, Mom," she said, turning around.

Whoops. No, it wasn't.

The look on her mom's face was definitely of the "Not-Okay" variety. In fact, it was deeply into "Over-My-Dead-Body" territory.

"Mo-*om*, I just need to use someone's computer."

"Is yours broken?"

"I need a Mac."

"We have chopped sirloin in the freezer."

Kirsten groaned in frustration. "I already *told* Virgil — "

"*Virgil?* I had no idea there was a Virgil in your life."

"*Ohhhhhh!*" Kirsten stormed back into the house. "What am I, a prisoner?"

"Call it whatever you want, but on the day after someone your own age has been killed in the neighborhood, you just may notice a *little* parental concern." As Kirsten huffed past, her mom's eyes narrowed. "Kirsten, what happened to your hand?"

"I cut it trying to get off my handcuffs!"

She went inside and slammed the front door behind her.

It took a few minutes for the steam to empty from her ears — just in time for Nat to return home to an even louder lecture from Mom.

Kirsten escaped upstairs, called Virgil, told

him about the disk, and explained that she'd been grounded.

Virgil responded with a deep sigh. "It's okay with me, but I don't know how I'm going to explain this to Wolfgang."

"Who?"

"My Mac. He's very sensitive. Especially when it gets close to the full moon. Often bad news makes him boot."

"Ha ha." Everybody was a comedian today.

"Don't worry, Kirsten. Just bring the disk to school tomorrow. We'll use the Macs there."

"Okay. Thanks, Virgil."

"You bet. Bye."

As she hung up, she heard her dad's voice outside, joining Mom's safety harangue against Nat.

Kirsten went downstairs. When she heard her dad starting to *defend* Nat, she decided to barge in. "Hi, Dad!" she called, stepping out the front door.

"Hey, sweetheart. I have something for you." He reached into his briefcase and pulled out a manila envelope. "That list, for your school project."

Eureka. Possible progress.

"Thanks!" Kirsten grabbed the envelope and went back inside.

She opened it in her room, sprawled on the bed. The heading read:

SOUTH OAKS COMMUNITY HOSPITAL E. R. OUTPATIENT ADMITTING

J. RANDALL, R.N., ATTENDING NURSE

NAME	AGE	TIME	COMPLAINT

Not too many people had signed in early in the day, but the number increased later on.

Olaf had been watching the Mets when his car was stolen — between 8:00 P.M. and 10:30 or so, assuming it was being played at home or at least on the East Coast.

Kirsten turned pages until she reached the one where 8:00 P.M. was listed.

Tons of people had signed in — for cuts, seizures, broken bones, drug overdoses, you name it. None of the names looked familiar.

That made sense. Kirsten hardly *knew* anyone in town. A classmate of hers could have been one of the patients and she wouldn't know it. This was ridiculous.

Her eyes stopped at 11:03. Three people had signed in — ages 43, 18, and 17. Their names were Smith, Jones, and Johnson. The nurse had written "Head and body injuries, torn clothing, fist fight."

Kirsten called the hospital and asked for Nurse Randall.

"I'm sorry," the receptionist said, "but she's out until tomorrow afternoon. Can someone else help you?"

"No, thanks."

Kirsten set the receiver down and sighed. Smith, Jones, and Johnson. Who were they? Three rough bozos with extremely average names.

Or three rough bozos who couldn't think of better ones.

Kirsten was still awake when her digital clock ticked to 3:00 A.M. The moon was almost full, and even with her shades *and* curtains drawn, it was too light inside.

Well, not *light*, exactly, but the room had kind of a dull glow.

Her desk lamp looked like an overgrown mushroom, her computer screen like a screaming mouth. The shag carpet seemed to be a bed of worms, waiting silently to devour Kirsten's feet.

Stop it. GO TO SLEEP!

She turned toward her wall and slammed her face into her pillow.

Scrunching her eyes tight, she willed herself to think of nothing. *Blackness. Absence of thought.*

"*Ohhhhh . . .*"

Kirsten was in no mood for mind games. She gave her jumpy brain a mental slap. *SLEEP!*

"*Ohhhhh . . .*"

Whack!

A door had slammed open against a wall. In her room.

Behind her.

"Dad?" she whimpered. "Mom? Natty, p-p-please don't scare me."

"*OHHHHH . . .*"

Kirsten jumped. The moan was practically in her ear. She spun around.

A human form loomed over her. Glowing with something other than light, something more like the incandescence of a dream.

At first Kirsten saw only the outline of clothing, tattered, blackened, and papery.

Then it staggered a step closer, struggling to open its mouth.

No. Not a mouth. A half-closed opening, caked with wet, gummy flesh and shards of

146

white tooth. Above the opening were two nostrils, like raisins set at the bottom end of a twisted stalk. Where eyes should have been were swollen puffs, pushed away from each other by an expanse of ripped skin that exposed a white, wrinkled, gelatinous ooze.

Its right hand was pointing to its throat repeatedly.

"*OHHHHHHHHHHH!*"

It took a step closer, its thin body struggling to stay up, stumbling over the ragged stumps at the end of its ankles.

Kirsten opened her mouth to scream as the creature fell onto her bed.

Chapter 20

The creature roared in agony, lifting its head like a trapped animal, dropping loose, fleshy shreds onto Kirsten's sheets.

Kirsten's scream stuck in her throat and became a dry, strangled click. Her back pressed against the corner.

The monster thrashed blindly, wrapping itself in her top sheet, which oozed black stains that grew large and jagged.

Air. Kirsten needed air. She was hardly breathing. Her feet were sliding toward the monster as it pulled desperately at the bottom sheet.

She swallowed. Her eyelids drooped closed. Her muscles let go.

Before she hit the floor, she heard a noise that cut through her like a machete.

Then, blackness.

*　*　*

When she awoke, her open mouth was full of drool-moistened carpet. She sat up with a start.

The surrounding light was like a rude smack to the eyes. She squinted against it.

"Did you hurt yourself, honey?"

She felt her dad's strong, gentle fingers pushing the sweat-sticky strands of hair away from her face.

Slowly he came into focus, kneeling next to her mom, both sleep-lined faces concentrating on her every reaction.

Her top sheet was in a heap a few inches away. She grabbed it and pulled it toward her.

Not a mark was on it.

"I — I — " Kirsten stammered.

He was pointing to his throat. He wanted to say something. He was here.

I am not crazy!

"Another bad dream, huh?" her mother asked softly.

Kirsten clutched her sheet and nodded weakly.

"When you were little, I used to read to you after you had nightmares," her mom continued. "You wanted to hear *Goodnight Moon* over and over and over."

Kirsten nodded. " 'Good-night, nobody.' " She recited her favorite line of the book in a parched whisper, remembering how it made her feel. Saying good-bye to the dragon or giant that had scared her so. Putting it away for good. Turning it into nothing. Nobody.

But that was then.

What she saw tonight was not going to be put away so easily. She knew it. It wanted to tell her something. It needed her.

And until she could find out why, she would never be free.

"Come on," her mom urged, helping her onto her bed. "Let's regress a little."

Moments later, Kirsten found herself dozing off, under her sheets, to her mom's hushed reading of *Goodnight Moon*.

Soon the room was silent. And dark, except for a light in the open closet. Her parents had gone.

But Kirsten was not asleep. She turned, scanning the room, wondering whether she would sleep downstairs, when her foot brushed against something.

Her leg jerked up toward her chest. She waited until she could feel herself breathing steadily.

Then, slowly, she pulled back her sheet.

A small, ragged object lay near the foot of her bed. Flat. Black.

She reached down and took it in her hand.

It was a scorched piece of denim.

Chapter 21

". . . For the trumpet shall sound,
and the dead shall be raised incor-
ruptible, and we shall be changed.
Death is swallowed up in victory.
O Death, where is thy sting? O
Grave, where is thy victory?"

The preacher's words pierced through Kirsten, stronger than the bitterness of the
cloudy morning.

She choked back a sob, and her father put
his arm around her shoulder. About forty people stood around Rob's grave, most glum and
silent, a few crying. The smell of the freshly
dug soil gave a musty sweetness to the chill.
Next to Kirsten, Virgil and Maria were sniffling
softly. Across the way, Mr. Busk and another
male teacher each had an arm around a red-

faced woman who stood between them. The woman looked a lot like Mr. Busk (poor thing), only she wasn't sweating as much. Mrs. Maxson stood alone near the preacher, wearing an old woolen coat and shivering. She had wanted the burial to be quick, and it was.

The dead shall be raised incorruptible, and we shall be changed. . . . Kirsten knew the words were supposed to be hopeful. They promised that Rob would find a better life after dying.

But Kirsten had seen death last night. And it was far from incorruptible. Or victorious.

The specter was still fresh in her mind — although *fresh* didn't seem an appropriate description. The burned, festering flesh; the smashed, ruined features; the bitter yearning — this body was filled with a human soul, stung badly, restless, still needing something.

Still waiting for the trumpet.

And it had come to Kirsten for help.

Kirsten had to fight from thinking of the creature as *it*. She knew who he was.

Nguyen Trang was still wandering around the way he'd been at death. The way he was when they peeled him out of the car in the ravine.

Firmly stuck in her jeans pocket, Kirsten's

right hand was closed tightly around the ripped, burned cloth she'd found in her bed. As if to convince herself the vision was real.

She had studied it closely in the light. It was a part of a jacket collar, with a melted top button.

A denim jacket. Not black leather.

Nguyen had not been dressed like a kamikaze pilot the night Olaf's car was stolen. Olaf had seen someone else.

"Blessed are the dead . . ." The preacher was closing his Bible, looking around at the crowd, reciting by memory. ". . . that they may rest from their labors, for their works do follow after them."

"Amen," Kirsten said along with the congregation.

The gathered group began to mingle, sadly shaking hands and talking in hushed voices. Kirsten made her way around the gravesite, introducing her dad to anyone she recognized, wanting eventually to say *something* to Mrs. Maxson.

When she got to Mr. Busk, he was much nicer than she expected. "Hello, Kirsten," he said, taking her hand. "Are you all right? I'm sorry about yesterday. I wasn't myself, thinking about Rob and all. . . ."

"I'm okay," Kirsten replied. "Mr. Busk, this is my dad."

"My pleasure." Mr. Busk shook his hand and gestured to the other teacher, whose name Kirsten didn't remember. "This is Tim Randall, a phys ed teacher at the school, and my sister, Janice, who was crazy enough to marry him."

Everyone chuckled politely. The woman smiled warmly at Kirsten's dad. "I already know Dr. Wilkes from the hospital."

"Of *course!*" Kirsten's dad said. "I didn't recognize you without your nurse's uniform."

Over Mr. Busk's shoulder, Kirsten could see Maria beckoning her. Quickly Kirsten moved on, leaving her dad to talk to Mr. Busk and his cohorts.

When Kirsten finally offered her condolences to Mrs. Maxson, she knew right away where Rob had gotten his extraordinary eyes.

Maria and Virgil were waiting by the road that wound through the cemetery. Kirsten gave her dad a kiss and said good-bye.

"I'm going to drop off Janice Randall at the hospital," he said. "Can I give you guys a ride to school?"

"No, thanks, Dad," Kirsten replied. "It's so close."

"Okay, see you later. And . . . I'm sorry about your friend."

"Thanks."

As he left to go to his car, he was joined by Mr. Busk's sister.

And Kirsten's mind began working. Walking toward Maria and Virgil, she reached into her backpack.

Folded around Nguyen's floppy disk was the list of Emergency Room sign-ins. She pulled it out and flipped it open. She had circled three names:

J. SMITH	17	11:03 P.M.	Cuts, bruises; fist fight
R. JONES	18	11:03 P.M.	"
P. JOHNSON	43	11:03 P.M.	"

Kirsten turned to the front page and read the name of the attending nurse: J. RANDALL.

Perfect! Maybe Mrs. Randall could remember those three. Maybe she had some suspicions, too.

"You coming or what?" Maria called to her from the road.

Kirsten stuffed the list into her backpack and joined her friends.

* * *

They got to school in time for lunch period. As they headed for the computer lab, Virgil warned them, "Ruggiero's not here till last period, in case we need his help. Grimble handles free period, and he's useless. He could make the alphabet complicated. So we'll look at the disk ourselves."

Inside the lab, Virgil took Kirsten's disk and sat at a Mac. A few other students were busily at work, supervised by a confused-looking teacher.

"Okay . . . let me fiddle around with this and . . ."

He clicked the mouse a few times and stared bewilderedly at the screen. "This mouse isn't working right. Can you two get me another one from the supply cabinet?"

Maria and Kirsten rummaged around in an old metal file cabinet by the wall and took out another mouse. When they got back, Virgil's fingers were tap dancing over the keyboard.

"I couldn't wait," he explained.

He folded his fingers and stared at the screen, which showed absolutely nothing.

"You sure this is the right disk?" he asked Kirsten.

"Yes. It has his name on it. Why?"

"It's blank."

Kirsten's heart sank.

"Blank?" Kirsten repeated. "How can that be? Who would go through the trouble to hide a blank disk?"

Virgil shrugged. "The moisture behind the wall, the heat — anything could have affected the data."

"You mean, there might have been data, and it was erased?" Kirsten asked.

"Right," Virgil replied, removing the disk. "It's gone."

"Can you recover stuff like that?" Kirsten asked.

"Mr. Ruggiero might know how. I'll ask him during last period." Virgil removed the disk and stuck it in his jacket pocket.

"So what do we do now?" Kirsten asked.

"Eat," Virgil replied with a grin.

Kirsten made it through lunch and English. She was patient. Calm. But when she saw Mr. Ruggiero heading in the direction of the computer lab on her way to study hall, she lost it.

Maria had study hall the same period, and today they'd planned to meet in the library. Kirsten found her in the magazine section.

"I saw him," Kirsten announced in a whisper.

"Who?" Maria said.

"Mr. Ruggiero. He's going to the computer lab *now*."

"Virgil's got social studies this period — "

"Does he have the disk?" Kirsten pressed. "I can't *wait*, Maria."

"I think he put it in his jacket pocket, which is in his locker — "

"Ohhhhh!"

"What are you moaning about?"

"You said he was in social studies."

Maria grinned and flexed her fingers. "But he didn't take his locker with him."

She went to the librarian and somehow wangled a hall pass. Then she and Kirsten went straight to Virgil's locker.

Maria opened it with ease. Virgil's jacket was hanging on a hook, and she took out the disk. "He thinks I don't know the combination," she said with a giggle.

They raced to the computer lab. Mr. Ruggiero was hacking away inside, all by himself.

"Oh, *hi*! Boy, are we glad you're here!" Maria exclaimed. "Kirsten and I were working on a project, and some of the files got erased.

Our teacher let us come see you about it. Do you have a minute? It's an Apple disk."

"I'll see what I can do." Mr. Ruggiero took the disk and inserted it into the Mac that Virgil had been using.

"Maybe you should replace that mouse," Maria suggested. "It's defective."

Mr. Ruggiero clicked it a couple of times. "Seems okay now," he said. "Okay, let me run a utility program on this and see what we come up with. . . ."

He clicked away furiously, until the screen was filled with chicken scratch. "Looks like somebody was messing with the File Allocation Table. I think I can fix that."

After a few minutes, he got up out of the chair and gestured for Kirsten to sit. "Okay. It should work, but you'll need to reboot with the disk in the drive."

Kirsten sat down and booted up the computer. The hard drive whirred. Words flashed across the screen. A software name. A copyright warning. "It's working!" she squealed.

Finally the screen stopped flashing and a single message appeared:

WELCOME TO YOUR DISK, N. TRANG!
TO PROCEED, ENTER PASSWORD.

"Password?" Kirsten repeated.

"Oh, brother," Maria mumbled.

Mr. Ruggiero was sitting at his computer now. Over his shoulder he called, "You forgot your own password?"

Quickly Maria blurted, "We changed it . . . yesterday. I remember! Wasn't it . . ." She bent down and whispered into Kirsten's ear, *"Just try things."*

"Yeah, that was it!" Kirsten replied a little too loudly.

What had her software manual said about passwords? She had skimmed over the chapter, and almost nothing had stuck in her mind — except that you should choose something meaningful to you but to absolutely no one else.

Kirsten typed in NGUYEN and then pressed the Enter key.

TRY AGAIN, the screen taunted.

She tried TRANG.

Then VIETNAM.

PORT LINCOLN (Maria's suggestion).

ANCHOR.

He liked cars: FERRARI, PORSCHE, MIATA, ESCORT

He did magic tricks: HOUDINI, MAGIC, ABRACADABRA . . .

They tried words until the bell rang at the end of the period. "This is totally absurd," Maria said. "It could be anything — his favorite baseball player, his favorite color, what he likes to eat. . . . It's probably something like the Vietnamese word for Twinkie. I say give up."

Kirsten looked at her watch. "I'm going to stick with it a couple more minutes."

"Suit yourself. See you."

As Maria joined the stream of kids in the hallway, Kirsten stared at the screen.

TRY AGAIN.

She was so close! She owed it to Nguyen to do this. Even if his journal gave her nothing, he deserved the effort.

Besides, she didn't think she could deal with any more visits from him.

What was the name of that organization that sent the letter?

OUTREACH, she typed.

That didn't work either. Kirsten wondered where the forwarded letter was now. Somewhere between Port Lincoln and who-knew-where, carrying just the news the Trangs wanted to hear — that Nguyen's *entire* family was dead now.

The family that no one knew about. The family Nguyen probably longed for his whole life long. The late Mr. and Mrs. Haing.

Kirsten nearly sprang out of her chair.

Her fingers attacked the keyboard.

HAING.

The screen blanked.

The hard drive started chugging.

Kirsten stared in amazement as a full-color display appeared on the screen — all kinds of electronic doodads, surrounding the words, YO, NGUYEN, WHAT'S UP?

Below it was today's date and a small menu.

"Yes!" Kirsten shouted.

RIIIINNNNNG! went the bell for the start of the next period.

"Uh, don't you have class?" Mr. Ruggiero asked.

"One minute," Kirsten said.

Mr. Ruggiero sighed and mumbled something about "senioritis."

Nguyen's first entry was almost two years ago. It was all about cars. So was the next day's entry, and the next. The fourth day mentioned a good grade on a science exam.

It was a real snoozer, but Kirsten felt guilty reading it.

He's dead, Kirsten said to herself. *He's not going to get mad at you.*

And she didn't have to tell the ghost.

She scrolled ahead to April of this year. He had entries on the tenth, twelfth, fifteenth. . . .

APRIL 18.

Bingo.

Kirsten began to read:

> *Today stunk. School was OK, but I couldn't concentrate. Gwen again. (OF COURSE.) The latest? She's not sure she likes me. I KNEW IT! I'm getting so sick of this. I am such a fool. I TOLD her last week I thought she still liked Rob. "Rob? What a dork." THOSE WERE HER EXACT WORDS. LIAR!*
>
> *And after what I gave her. She'll never know what that meant to me. How could I be so stupid? How am I going to get it back?*
>
> *Oh, speaking of all this, guess who just called and wants to see me tonight?*

"Hey, what are you doing?"

Kirsten turned around in time to get Virgil's forearm across her shoulders. She lost her balance and fell to the floor.

Virgil hunched over the computer, staring wide-eyed at the screen, fumbling with the mouse.

"Virgil!" Kirsten cried.

"What's gotten into you, Garth?" Mr. Ruggiero bellowed. He pushed Virgil aside and helped Kirsten off the floor.

Virgil's face was red. "She *stole* that disk!" he shouted, his voice shrill and desperate.

Kirsten scrambled onto the chair and read the rest of Nguyen's entry:

> *Rob Maxson. I'm supposed to meet him on Riverside Drive. He says he found a Ferrari in the woods. Maybe I can talk to him about Gwen.*

Those were the last words Nguyen Trang wrote before he died.

Chapter 22

Virgil was on his knees now, shoulder to shoulder with Kirsten, reading the screen. His body slumped.

Kirsten looked at him when she finished. He looked deflated. Terrified.

"You know about this, don't you?" Kirsten asked.

Virgil swallowed. He glanced over his shoulder into the empty hallway. "Yeah."

Mr. Ruggiero glanced at the screen briefly, then said, "Are you two cool now? No more trouble?"

"We're all right," Kirsten replied.

As Mr. Ruggiero went back to his computer, Kirsten asked, "Want to go someplace to talk?"

"I have class," Virgil said.

"So do I. Come on, we're late already. A few more minutes won't hurt."

"Well . . ." Virgil pursed his lips nervously, ran his fingers through his hair. "All right. I guess. Let's go out the exit near the ball field."

He left the room first. When Kirsten followed, she caught a glimpse of Mr. Busk walking quickly away, down the long corridor to their left.

"How'd he get there?" Kirsten asked. "I didn't see him walk by."

Virgil shrugged. "How should I know? Come on."

They scooted down the hall and out the side door. Neither of them had coats, and the day hadn't turned any warmer since the burial. Kirsten felt her teeth chatter. She held the top of her blouse closed.

Virgil looked off in the distance, his knitted eyebrows creating a cleft down his forehead.

"Rob was involved in Nguyen Trang's death, wasn't he? That was why you didn't want me to read the disk. You were protecting him."

Virgil nodded.

"He was wearing his black leather jacket that night," Kirsten went on, "and he stole Olaf Maarten's car."

"Well . . . *a* black leather jacket. The one you're thinking about is new. The old one was destroyed . . ." Virgil swallowed hard and said in a barely audible voice, ". . . in the accident."

Kirsten leaned in close. "What happened that night, Virgil? You know, don't you?"

"Yes . . . I mean, *some* of it. Rob told me. We used to be buddies, but we . . . fell out. Anyway, he wanted to go for a joyride with someone who knew about cars — but he figured Nguyen would say no since he was so goody-goody. So he lied; managed to get Nguyen to come to Riverside Drive, where no one would see them. But all Nguyen wanted to do was talk about Gwen. They went driving, and Nguyen got angry, and . . ."

Virgil broked off. His eyes began to water.

"And what, Virgil?" Kirsten said gently. "Don't keep it in. They're both gone now. You can tell me everything."

Virgil sniffed back the tears. "I guess they were arguing too much, and you know that road, it's really bad in the rain, and . . . well, neither of them was wearing a seat belt, and when the car went over, Rob got thrown out. But Nguyen . . . wasn't so lucky."

"And Rob went to the hospital, didn't he? And checked in under a fake name."

Virgil looked surprised. "Yeah. How do you — "

"Was anyone else with him?"

"Not that I know of," Virgil said. "I mean, he didn't tell me everything."

"Virgil, *three* people checked in to the E.R. that night with cuts and bruises — and with the fakest-sounding aliases you can imagine. Rob had two more people with him. He lied to you!"

"I — well — wow . . . I guess I didn't know him as well as I thought."

Kirsten exhaled. "I guess a lot of people didn't."

She let her head fall on Virgil's shoulder. It felt stiff and cold.

Gwen was absent from driver's ed that day, but even so, the car felt even more miserable than usual.

No one wanted to talk. Mr. Busk barked out his commands in a monotone. When she wasn't driving, Sara stared out the window, listening to a Walkman. Even Maria was grim and quiet.

Kirsten couldn't stop thinking about Nguyen. *What did he want?* It couldn't be revenge; Rob was already dead. But there was something else, she was sure of it.

Kirsten's drive was pretty good, all things considered. She was last, and she managed to park the car in the lot without any trouble.

As she applied the parking brake, Sara and Maria scooted out of the backseat.

"Nice job, Kirsten," Mr. Busk said. "I wish I had you for a few more classes. You're so close to being ready." He shook his head sadly.

"But . . . you don't think I *am* ready."

"Well, you'll do all right on the written part, I'm sure, but . . ." He gazed out the window, then at his watch. "Do you have any extra-curriculars today?"

"No."

"Hmmmm. You see that car over there?"

Kirsten looked out the window at an old, shiny, black Chevy parked near the auto shop. "That one?"

"It used to belong to a friend of mine who lived in New York City. Instead of junking it, he gave it to us. Anyway, we fixed it up in shop and I was going to test-drive it myself. But maybe I won't. Maybe I'll let you do it."

"Me — *now?* Why?"

"I'm offering you some extra time. My own time. I know I'm not the most considerate guy, but I see how hard you've been working — and I owe you something after I yelled at you yesterday." He shrugged. "But, hey, I know it's an unfamiliar car and if you don't want to — "

"That's okay!" Kirsten cut in. "I'll do it."

So close to being ready. Kirsten thought she was hearing things. Not long ago Mr. Busk had told her she was going to flunk. Had she really gotten better? Was he kidding?

Was he drunk? Kirsten glanced at him as he walked to the Chevy. He wasn't *weaving*, but you never knew.

As Kirsten got out, she spotted Maria chatting with Virgil in the driveway. She caught Maria's attention and waved her arm, as if to say, "You go ahead."

Then she opened the door of the Chevy and thought she would barf.

The ashtray was spilling over with cigarette butts. An ancient paper cup, half filled with stale coffee, was perched on the windshield next to three-quarters of a ham-and-cheese sandwich reeking of rancid mustard.

"Uh, let me get rid of the junk," Mr. Busk said sheepishly.

Kirsten waited as he quickly emptied the garbage from the car, then went over the surfaces with a rag and cleaning fluid.

Before she stepped in, she picked up a *Sports Illustrated* swimsuit calendar that was lying on top of a red, metal, antitheft steering-wheel bar on the floor.

As Kirsten tossed the calendar in the back, Mr. Busk explained, "That Club belonged to the guy who owned this before. He had *everything* in this car — alarm, hood lock, the works."

Kirsten sat in the driver's seat and looked at all the switches and red lights that had been attached to the dashboard. Typical New York City car, armed against theft — complete with a key-operated ignition shutoff exactly like her dad's. When you pushed in the button, the car could not be started. This car's button was under the glove compartment, though — her dad's had been near the steering column.

"Okay, ready when you are, Kirsten," Mr. Busk said.

Kirsten started up and drove out of the lot. This car had a lot more power than the driver's ed cars she'd been used to, and she liked the feel of it.

"Good start. Okay, turn left."

Mr. Busk guided her through the nearby side streets, practicing K-turns, starting and stopping, signaling, parallel parking.

Then they went to Sunrise Highway, which ran alongside the commuter train tracks. There, on long stretches of uninterrupted highway, Kirsten practiced lane changing and passing.

"Kirsten, I am shocked," Mr. Busk said while they were stopped at a light. "I never thought you'd make it. But you know what? I'm not supposed to tell you this, but I'm going to pass you."

"Really?"

"Yep. Now," he said, peering over her head to the left, "turn left and go over the train tracks."

Kirsten was ready to burst. After the last two horrific days, this was the best news she'd heard. She couldn't help smiling as she made the turn.

In the distance, she heard a train approaching.

"Okay, the gate's open, Kirsten. That train isn't as close as it seems. What do you do?"

Kirsten had made the turn. She was crossing the oncoming-car-traffic lanes, where the cars were stopped for a red light. A few yards beyond Sunrise, the tracks crossed the road. She had room enough to stop and wait.

Honnnnk!

She saw a car in her rearview mirror, so close she could swear it was touching.

"Ignore that jerk," Mr. Busk said. "Just go over the tracks, carefully and *slowly*."

Kirsten put her foot on the brakes. As she approached the tracks, the car slowed way down. The train was getting louder now, but Mr. Busk didn't seem too concerned.

The car behind her whizzed by on the right, careening over the tracks. "To you, too, buddy!" the driver shouted to Mr. Busk as he passed, then swerved to cut Kirsten off, tossing off an obscene gesture.

Kirsten jammed on the brake. She gave Mr. Busk a quick glance. His right hand was out the window.

Kirsten looked ahead. She stepped on the gas but the car didn't move. She checked the gear shift and the emergency brake, and gassed it again.

The engine made a gagging noise, then stopped.

Clack . . . clack . . . clack . . .

Kirsten looked to the left. She could *see* the train now.

Ca-chunk.

The gate in front of her slammed down. Red lights flashed. No other cars were at the intersection.

"Mr. Busk?"

He was running. Bailing out. Slamming the door behind him and racing away. His window, which had been open a moment before, was closed.

Kirsten grabbed the handle of her door. It was locked. She felt around for the lock, but it was electronic. She needed battery power.

She turned the key. Nothing.

She dove across the seat and pulled the handle of Mr. Busk's door.

He had locked it!

HOOOONNNNNNNNK!

The train's horn blasted. Its brakes sounded like a chorus of shrieking witches. The front gleamed silver, growing, filling her window.

Desperately Kirsten looked for an escape. Her eyes passed across the ignition shutoff switch under the glove compartment.

It had been pressed in.

And Mr. Busk had the keys.

Kirsten was trapped.

Chapter 23

Kirsten banged on the window, the windshield. She screamed. She lay on her back and tried to *kick* out the side window.

She pushed against the floor with her hand to brace herself for a stronger kick.

Her fingers wrapped around the Club.

EEEEEEEEEEEEEEEEE —

The train's brakes let out a deafening shriek.

She sat up. She lifted the Club to her shoulder and swung.

It thudded dully against the passenger-side window.

With a cry of desperation, she swung again.

CRAAASSSSSHHHH!

The window shattered. Kirsten dived through it. She heard a ripping noise. She landed on her shoulder and rolled away from the car. Scrambling to her feet, she ran.

She got as far as a scrubby hedge beyond the north side of the tracks when the train hit.

The noise shook the ground. The car crumpled like a toy and shot forward. In a sickening scream of scraping metal, the snub nose of the locomotive pushed the black wreckage along the tracks.

Fifty yards later, train and car finally stopped in a cloud of acrid smoke.

Kirsten stared at the twisted, flattened remains of the car. A moment more, and she would have been in there.

He tried to kill me.

She let the idea sink in. Mr. Busk wanted her dead. He had made her go over the tracks, closed the windows, and pressed the shutoff button.

And he had been careful enough not to ruin a driver's ed car while killing her.

She looked at herself for the first time. Her pants were torn. Her right arm had a bleeding gash along its entire length. Her cheek stung where her face had hit the ground.

But Kirsten felt rooted to the spot. She didn't move until she saw ambulance lights flashing.

The vehicle came to a screeching halt and two white-suited men rushed out toward the smashed car. A crowd of gawkers had already formed. Their eyes were glued to the accident, but it wouldn't be long before someone turned her way.

Kirsten got up. Pain shot from her left ankle all the way up her back. She made tracks away from Sunrise as fast as her aching legs could take her.

"What happened to *you*?" said Nat as she limped into the house.

"I fell," Kirsten said.

"Where? Into a trash compacter?"

Kirsten went into the bathroom, closed the door, and looked in the mirror.

What she saw was *not* pretty. Her face was scraped, but it had already stopped bleeding. The arm and leg were much worse. She took off her clothes and showered, gritting her teeth against the pain.

Afterward she carefully covered the open wounds with gauze. Then she wrapped a towel around her, went upstairs, and changed.

She hobbled into her parents' room and called Maria.

"Maria, hi, I have to talk to you."

"What's wrong, Kirsten? Mr. Busk tried to put the moves on you? You attract all the winners, don't you?"

"No! Listen to me, *(boop!)* I — "

Call waiting. Of all the times to be interrupted!

"He took me driving — in another car — and he tried to — *(boop!)* Ohhhhh!"

"Take the call, Kirsten. I'll be here."

Kirsten clicked the receiver hook. "Hello!" she snapped.

"Kirsten! Thank God you're home." It was Virgil, speaking in a rushed, pinched whisper. "Meet me right away, at Riverside and West. Don't talk to anybody. Don't let anything stop you."

"But I'm on the phone with Maria — "

"Get rid of her."

"But — "

"Kirsten, this involves your life. Get rid of Maria and don't tell her I called. *Now!*"

"Okay." She clicked the hook again. "Hi, Maria! Listen, I have to go. Can I call you later?"

"You're going to leave me hanging like this? What could be so important — "

"See you, Maria. Sorry. Bye."

Click.

She limped downstairs and out to the garage. Nat was playing Nintendo in the den and ignored her.

As she lifted her right leg over her bike, she grimaced in agony. But the pain was dull and throbbing, not sharp like a bone break. She could make it.

She pushed off with her good foot and began rolling. Girding herself, she pedaled down the driveway and into the street.

Kirsten went straight to Riverside Drive, which ran along the west side of Port Lincoln. Toward the edge of town, the houses she passed were larger and farther apart. Port Lincoln became almost rural here, until it disappeared entirely into forest beyond West Street.

But Riverside Drive kept going, all the way to Fenimore Village. Years ago it was the *only* road that led to Fenimore, until the parkway was built and people could make the trip in three minutes. Riverside had become a cracked, potholed, country road twisting through pines and maples that seemed to grow closer to the blacktop every year. It followed the Sagramore River for a while, then crossed over it on a stone bridge.

It was near that stone bridge that Nguyen Trang had lost his life.

As Kirsten approached West Street, the sun was setting to her left. It had recently burned away the clouds, just in time to make the leaves overhead look like a canopy of flames. Two blocks from the intersection, she could see Virgil's silhouette. He was pacing, looking up West Street.

She was about to shout to him, but she didn't.

A red Jeep appeared, speeding from West Street into the intersection. It squealed to a halt, and Mr. Busk got out.

Kirsten squeezed her hand brake. Quickly she got off her bike and hid behind a nearby hedge.

"What are you doing *here*?" Mr. Busk bellowed.

Virgil stammered an answer Kirsten couldn't hear.

Mr. Busk did not seem happy with the answer, and he began looking up and down Riverside. Lowering his voice, he argued with Virgil, gesturing angrily with his arms.

Virgil looked terribly anxious.

They were waiting for me. This was a setup.

The thought ripped its way into her consciousness. She never would have suspected Virgil.

But Virgil had called her immediately after Busk had tried to kill her.

And Virgil had gone *ballistic* when he'd seen her reading Nguyen's disk. *A defective mouse?* How could Kirsten have been so stupid? Mr. Ruggiero had said the mouse was fine. Virgil had lied so he could sabotage the disk while she and Maria went off rummaging in the file cabinet.

And Mr. Busk had been in the hallway when they'd left the lab.

They were working together. But *why?* What did *they* have to do with Nguyen and Rob?

Kirsten's jaw dropped with a sudden realization.

43, 18, 17.

Those were the ages of "Johnson," "Jones," and "Smith."

The ages (more or less) of Mr. Busk, Rob, and Virgil.

And no one at the hospital checked IDs. No one was suspicious. Why?

Because the attending nurse was Mr. Busk's sister.

Kirsten heard a slam. She looked toward the Jeep. Mr. Busk was rushing to get into the driver's side. Virgil was nowhere in sight.

With a roar and a cloud of black smoke, the Jeep disappeared up Riverside Drive.

Chapter 24

Kirsten hopped on her bike. Her pain was gone. She could feel her blood pulsing wildly at her temples.

She pedaled furiously. Beneath her, fallen leaves crackled under her tires.

As she followed the first sharp bend in the road, her tires slipped. She skidded left, sticking out her leg to stop the fall.

She bounced back upright and continued. Her eyes scanned the blacktop in front of her for leaves. She steered around the thickest piles. She could not afford to fall over now.

But the bike was no match for a Jeep. Kirsten saw no sign of it. The engine noise soon died out. Mr. Busk was probably driving along the outskirts of Fenimore Village, heading for the parkway.

She continued a while longer, but finally stopped.

Her breaths came in savage gulps; her throat was parched and dry. She felt unstable as she propped her bike on a pine tree and sat on an old log.

She had lost him. Years ago, after the war, Mr. Busk had vanished once from Port Lincoln. Now he was likely to vanish for good.

And no one would know that he had helped destroy Nguyen Trang.

Now Kirsten knew what Nguyen had wanted. Vengeance.

He had gotten it from Rob. Now he wanted the other two. Somehow they were involved in his death.

As the harsh hacksawing of her own breaths diminished, Kirsten began noticing the sounds around her. The screech of a chipmunk. The skittering of a squirrel. The dropping of acorns. The caw of crows. The lapping of the river below her.

The chugging of a balky car engine.

Yes. The sound was unmistakable.

Kirsten rose to her feet. Below her, a dirt path wound along the riverbank. Silently, on the sides of her feet, she descended the gentle slope and followed the path toward the noise.

The river took a sharp left less than a hundred yards ahead. Kirsten trained her eye upward. Through the crisscrossing tree trunks and blowing leaves, she caught a glint of metal.

Carefully she edged closer. When she could see the road clearly, she hid behind a sycamore tree.

Whirrrr . . . whirrrr . . . chock-chock!

Mr. Busk's Jeep had veered off the road. Its right bumper had hit a tree, and now the engine wasn't starting.

She heard Mr. Busk's voice muttering epithets she'd never even heard before. He pushed his door open, got out, and kicked the door shut again in frustration.

Standing with hands on hips, he looked down Riverside Drive.

Kirsten ducked behind the tree.

Soon she heard footsteps tapping on the road . . . crunching on leaves and fallen branches . . . coming nearer.

"Hey. Who's there?"

Kirsten froze.

"Come on, get out. I see you. You got a car?"

Kirsten took a deep breath and stepped out.

Mr. Busk stopped in his tracks. His jaw dropped open. "*K-Kirsten?*"

"Did you think I was dead?" she asked.

"Well, I — I saw — the train — " He swallowed and cleared his throat. "I was so worried. I — I bailed out when I saw that gate go down, and I knew you'd do the same. But then, I wasn't sure. I didn't see you afterward. . . ."

"I got out. I rolled away on the other side of the tracks."

"Well, thank God you're alive!"

"Yeah. I sure don't have *you* to thank."

Mr. Busk stepped backward, up the slope. "What do you mean?"

"Oh, you didn't know?" Kirsten followed him, step for step. "I guess you closed the window before you jumped to avoid a last-minute chill — and your knee nicked the ignition shutoff by accident on your way out. I'm not sure why you went through the trouble to lock the door, though. . . ."

Now Mr. Busk's back was to the rear end of the Jeep. He stopped. "Kirsten, I don't know what you're talking about. I — I called to you! I yelled, 'Push your door open!' I mean, the train was pretty loud by then. . . ."

Behind Mr. Busk, Kirsten spotted movement in the Jeep's rear window. Slowly, Virgil rose into view, his face covered with blood.

His eyes locked with Kirsten's for a split second.

The expression on Mr. Busk's face flickered with instant understanding. He spun around.

Whack!

The Jeep's rear door flew open, catching Mr. Busk in the chest.

He staggered backward. His foot caught a patch of leaves on the lip of the road.

Windmilling his arms, he fell.

"Hurry!" Virgil urged, pulling the door shut again.

Kirsten raced to the driver's side. She yanked open the door and hopped inside. The key was in the ignition.

Whirrrrrr . . . whirrrrr!

Flooded. The engine was flooded. That was what Rob had called that noise. *What were you supposed to do?*

"He's coming!" Virgil yelled from the back of the Jeep.

Kirsten locked the door. Mr. Busk's shirt filled the side mirror. Now he was grabbing the door handle.

Suddenly Kirsten remembered. She turned the key without touching the gas pedal.

Whirrrrrr . . . whirrrrr . . . ka-CHOOOOOM!

The Jeep roared to life.

"*OPEN THE DOOR!*" Mr. Busk howled beside her.

"*Go! GO!*" Virgil yelled.

Kirsten looked at the dashboard in a panic. She had never driven a Jeep. Everything was in the wrong place.

But she couldn't think about that. She pulled the shift down to Drive. Then she trained her eyes on the road, yanked the steering wheel to the left, and floored the gas pedal.

The tires left the dirt and connected with the road. And Kirsten felt the crash of shattering glass near her head.

Chapter 25

"GO!" Virgil's voice was a high-pitched wail.

Kirsten screamed and flinched as shards of glass fell against her. Some stuck to her hair, some tinkled to the floor.

She pressed her foot down hard, but the Jeep was swerving out of control.

The window beside her was a jagged hole. But she was unhurt.

She sat up. Her eyes widened. She was heading for an outcropping of solid rock along the other side of the road. Fast.

"We're going to die!" Virgil cried.

Kirsten pulled the steering wheel to the right. The Jeep felt as if it were going to keel over.

Then they were on the road. Moving. The blacktop stretched out ahead, mottled with swirling eddies of fallen leaves.

"Stop!" shouted a distant voice.

In the rearview mirror, Kirsten saw Mr. Busk rearing back with a large rock. He let fly.

CRONK!

It hit the roof with a loud, explosive, metallic sound.

But Kirsten kept her eyes forward. Her hands on the wheel. Her foot on the gas.

And in moments, Mr. Busk was an agitated speck in the mirror, disappearing around a bend in the road.

"Yeeeeee-hahhh!" Virgil yelled.

Kirsten grinned. Now this — *this* was a drive!

A couple of miles later Kirsten had to slow down. For one thing, it was getting dark and the old country road had no lights. For another, this section had some treacherous turns.

"Whoa . . . stop," Virgil piped up.

He was now sitting in the passenger seat, staring out his window.

"Why?" Kirsten asked.

"This is the place," he said. "This is where Nguyen died."

Kirsten applied the brake and stopped at the

side of the road. As she shifted to Park, she gazed out at the steep ravine beyond a thick concrete guardrail.

"They crashed through *that*?" Kirsten asked.

Virgil shook his head. "That was put up after the accident. A metal railing used to be there. Rob clipped the end of it."

"Rob?" Kirsten stared at Virgil. "So *Rob* was driving, not Nguyen."

Virgil's head lowered. "Yeah. I guess."

"You *guess*?" Fury exploded from Kirsten. "Damn it, Virgil. You lured me into a trap, and what did I do? Leave you with Mr. Busk, where you belonged? No. I may have just saved your life. And for what? You've been lying to me every step of the way! I know you were involved in the accident, Virgil. So don't *guess*. I swear, if you hold back from me anymore, I will haunt you the rest of your worthless life."

Or someone else will.

"No . . . no." Virgil was shaking his head. "I didn't lure you, Kirsten. I was trying to save you. To warn you. Mr. Busk called to tell me you'd been hit. He made it sound like it was your fault. He was, like, hyperventilating over the phone. He wanted to meet me, but *not* at

West and Riverside. When I called and found out you were alive, I suspected Mr. Busk had tried to kill you. Before I went to meet him, I wanted to tell you the truth — away from your house, in case he checked. I knew he'd gone off the deep end. He'd been acting strange lately. He knew you were about to blow open our alibi. His sister had told him you were snooping around with the E.R. records — "

"Alibi for *what*, Virgil? What happened here?"

Virgil's eyes glazed over. He started breathing heavily. "I vowed I'd never talk about this. I wanted to forget it. I thought . . . I thought it would go away."

"It'll never go away, Virgil."

"I know . . . I know." He began speaking in slow, measured tones, his eyes moistening. "Rob had it in for Nguyen — he was convinced Mr. Trang stole his dad's job, and *that* was why his dad had abandoned the family. But that wasn't true. Mr. Maxson was fired because he was a drunk. And he'd been fighting with Mrs. Maxson for years. Anyway, Rob knew I liked Gwen, and he got it in his mind that he would scare Nguyen away from Gwen — for my sake, he said. That was what this whole thing was about. It wasn't really for *me*; it was just an excuse to torment Nguyen."

"So he *killed* him?"

"No. He wanted to frighten him, take him on a dangerous ride and threaten him. Maybe let him out in the woods without his clothes — something stupid like that. He thought that would be fun. I don't know why he wanted me to come. I don't know why I agreed. But before I knew it, there we were, tooling along in the rain. Nguyen was in the middle, trapped between us. We were slipping and sliding, and . . . a car came in the other direction, in the wrong lane. Rob swerved into the guardrail, and the car went over. Somehow Rob was thrown clear. His jacket was destroyed, but he wasn't badly hurt. I was wearing a seat belt, but Nguyen wasn't. His head smashed into the windshield. Hard.

"I blacked out, until Rob pulled me from the wreckage. Nguyen was dead; we checked him. Then . . . then we panicked. We were worried someone would find out. So we — "

Virgil's voice broke off. A sudden, choked sob erupted from him, and he began weeping.

Kirsten waited a moment. She couldn't bring herself to comfort him.

"We moved him," Virgil continued.

"What do you mean, *moved* him?" Kirsten asked.

"Into the driver's seat. To make it look like he was driving. Alone. Then Rob started freaking out about fingerprints. He wanted me to go in and start wiping all the surfaces. We argued and argued, and suddenly . . ." Virgil took a breath and stared out the window. "Suddenly we heard an explosion. It knocked us off our feet. When we looked back, the car had burst into flames."

Kirsten sat back in her seat. She let the horrible tale sink in. She sifted through the details, wondering how such a thing could have happened.

"Virgil," she said, "what about the car that ran you off the road? Did you find out who it was?"

Virgil shrugged. "A drunk driver."

"A drunk driver?"

"Yeah."

"Did he happen to be driving a red Jeep?"

Virgil looked away.

Kirsten's head was pounding. "Busk killed the wrong person that night, Virgil," she said through clenched teeth. "You and Rob were lucky. You could have at least reported Busk. But what did you do? *You helped him cover up the murder of your own classmate!*"

"We had no choice!" Virgil's voice was a harsh, pleading whine. "Busk said the accident was Rob's fault — and if we all didn't cover it up, he'd tell the cops *Rob* caused the accident."

"But he was drunk. A cop would know — "

"*He's a driver's ed teacher, Kirsten!* And Rob was driving a stolen car. Who do you think the cops would believe?"

Kirsten stared straight ahead. "Tell me. Was Busk sober enough to drive you to the hospital, or did Rob drive?"

After a silence that seemed to last an hour, Virgil mumbled, "Rob drove."

"So that was that, huh? You thought you pulled it off — until Maria told you I was starting to get interested in Nguyen. Was that why you came to my house? You were coming on to me, Virgil. Was that part of the plan, too?"

"I — I knew the Trangs had moved without finding Nguyen's diary," Virgil said. "I got worried that you would. Rob had been worried about that, too. So I figured I'd become your . . . friend. Maybe I'd find the diary first."

"You left the attic door open!" Kirsten blurted out. "When you were taking that long time in the upstairs bathroom . . ."

"I wasn't in the bathroom at all. I was snooping around — you know, looking for loose floorboards, hidden cracks, anyplace a book might fit. I hadn't thought it'd be on a disk. Anyway, I was in your room when I heard that crash downstairs."

The plate. The door had swung open, knocked it over, and created a distraction.

Kirsten mumbled, "Nguyen . . ."

"What?"

Telekinesis. When you move things by thinking about them. Those had been Maria's words. Joking about Nguyen.

Some joke.

Kirsten's mind was racing. If he could move a plate, could he . . . ? "He took Rob. He's going to take you, Virgil. Maybe Gwen, too. And me. Maybe everybody, until he gets what he wants!"

Virgil looked at her as if she'd completely lost it. "What are you talking about? *Who?*"

"Just hear me, Virgil. You don't have to believe a word. I thought Gwen had killed Rob, but she didn't. Nguyen is trying to get revenge. The picture of the Escort on that

196

driver's ed contest flyer — it moves. Slowly. It turns toward you a little at a time, and then — "

"And then what? It drives off the page?"

"Rob had a flyer with him the night he died. I found it the next day. The car was missing, Virgil."

"Oh my God . . . oh my God . . ."

"I know you think I'm crazy, but — "

Virgil shook his head. "That's not why I'm saying that. Look in the back, Kirsten."

Kirsten craned her neck.

A manila envelope sat on the backseat. It was labeled CONTEST FLYERS.

Chapter 26

"What do we do with them?" Virgil asked.

"I don't know," Kirsten replied.

"Throw them out?" Virgil reached into the back.

"Don't touch them!" Kirsten snapped. "We don't know what might happen."

"Is the . . . mechanism, the spell, *whatever* you call it — is it activated if the flyer's inside an envelope?"

"I — I don't know."

"Or does it have to do with, like, personal possession? In other words, only if it actually belongs to you — "

"Virgil, how should I know?"

Virgil reached for the handle. "Well, I don't know about you, but I'm getting out of here."

"No, don't!" Kirsten said. "Mr. Busk is out

there somewhere. He's probably coming after us. It's already getting too dark to go home through the woods. We can drive into Fenimore Village and circle home using the expressway."

"But the flyers — "

"They haven't done anything to us yet. It'll be only ten minutes to get home the long way. Let's take the chance. We can ditch the Jeep when we get into Port Lincoln."

"Okay, fine. But if I get run over while we're in here, you're in trouble!" Virgil sank back into his seat. "Wait a minute. If we're *in* a car, can another car materialize inside it? And if it does, would the surrounding car inhibit its growth, or . . ."

Kirsten let him ramble on as she shot down Riverside Drive.

By the time she wound through Fenimore Village and found the expressway, Virgil had fallen silent.

Kirsten clutched the steering wheel, staying carefully in the right lane at forty miles an hour. She *hated* expressway driving. Cars hurtled by her like rockets.

"Kirsten?" Virgil finally said.

"This is as fast as I'm going to go!" she retorted.

Virgil didn't seem to hear the comment. "Maybe Nguyen is a revenant."

"Huh?"

"You know . . . a restless spirit. I saw a show about this once. It's someone who dies before he's supposed to, and he can't die in peace unless he gets something that he really wanted before he died. They need, like, some tribal headdress, or a picture of their newborn baby, or — "

"Virgil, I'm trying to concentrate — "

"Sorry — "

Suddenly Kirsten slammed on the brakes and veered into the breakdown lane. She came to a full stop and turned to Virgil. "What did you say?"

"I said, 'Sorry.' "

"I mean, before that. About the revenants."

"I was just mouthing off. I don't know, it was just a TV movie — "

Kirsten cut him off. "Virgil, did Nguyen wear any jewelry?"

"Jewelry? Like an earring or something? I don't think so. He was pretty conservative."

"Like around his neck? He kept pointing to his neck."

"Who?"

"Just answer my question!"

Virgil shut up and thought. "Well . . . hm. Yeah. Actually, he did. This grungy old thing. Like a . . . pendant, or whatever."

"A locket?"

"Yeah, I guess you call it that — "

Kirsten gunned the accelerator.

"Hey, easy!" Virgil protested. "What'd I say?"

"Hang on."

By the time Kirsten parked the Jeep on Main Street, the sun had set. The street lamp in front of Something Old, Something New was dead, and the shop window glowed eerily with its low-wattage lightbulbs.

She left her door open as she ran to the window and peered in.

The display had been rearranged. A few leaves had been strewn haphazardly around, probably to create an autumn motif. A laptop computer was the centerpiece, and to its left was the small, felt-covered, slanted shelf holding jewelry.

Right in the center was the locket Gwen had traded in.

"What are you looking for?" asked Virgil, sidling up beside her.

Before Kirsten could respond, Virgil said,

"Hey, that's it! That's Nguyen's pendant!"

Kirsten stared at it in disbelief. It was small and old and unremarkable, carved with lines that had faded over the years.

"That's *it*?" Kirsten murmured under her breath. *"That's what all this is about?"*

It seemed so . . . trivial. So needless. Someone had died — and for what? A stupid, tarnished little trinket?

Kirsten looked carefully at the window. Silver burglar-sensor tape surrounded the edges. She would have to work fast.

"Uh, I think it's closed," Virgil volunteered. "I could try to, like, slip a credit card into the door latch. I saw someone do that on TV — "

"Uh-uh," Kirsten said, running back to the Jeep. "I think I know an easier way."

She flicked on the Jeep's inside light and felt around under the seat.

"You're not going to drive into the window?" Virgil asked.

"I hope not." Under the passenger seat, Kirsten found what she wanted. She pulled it out and smiled. "I *figured* he had one of these."

Mr. Busk's Club was the deluxe version, even heavier than the one she'd used before. "Ever seen one of these?" she asked Virgil.

"I don't think you have to worry about car theft, Kirsten. We're right here."

Kirsten approached the window, rearing back with the Club.

"What are you doing?" Virgil asked.

"Get away," Kirsten replied. "I'm good at this."

With a sharp swing, she sent the Club flying through the center of the pawnshop window.

BRIIIIIIIINNNNNNG!

The alarm echoed up and down the deserted street.

Kirsten reached through the gaping hole, grabbed the locket, and ran.

Chapter 27

"Let's go!" Kirsten stuffed the locket in her pocket and jumped into the Jeep.

Virgil was cemented to the sidewalk, gawking.

"Come on!" Kirsten insisted.

Finally he broke away. His footsteps crunching the broken glass, he ran to the Jeep and climbed into the other side. "Where to now?"

"I don't know!"

She drove blindly through the darkened streets of Port Lincoln. The sound of police sirens now rang out. Kirsten would have to be careful. She was in a stolen car, driving without a license, having just vandalized a store. For all she knew, her mom may have called the cops to report her missing, too.

"I hate to say this, Virgil, but I think we'd

better leave town." Kirsten steered the Jeep toward the entrance to the expressway.

"Great. Just great, Kirsten. I had a promising life ahead of me, you know, and now — "

"Cram it, Virgil! You're not smelling like a rose yourself — "

A flash of red-and-white lights darted across the next intersection.

"Oh, wonderful," Virgil said. "They're going our way."

"Maybe they're blocking the expressway," Kirsten remarked.

"So take Riverside!"

Kirsten did a K-turn, using someone's driveway. She drove back west, hooking up with Riverside Drive at the edge of town.

Before long they were back where they'd started, driving toward Fenimore Village.

"Kirsten, we're fugitives!" Virgil cried out. "Our faces will be hanging in post offices coast to coast. We won't be able to stop for gas. What are we going to do — drive around till we find a plastic surgeon who can change our looks for free?"

"Just let me think, okay?" Kirsten retorted.

"What if we see Mr. Busk?"

"He'd better get out of the way!"

But they didn't see him. Not along the river, not over the bridge, nowhere.

Thoughts caromed inside Kirsten's brain. *What now? Do I go home with the locket and wait for Nguyen? How will I explain the injuries? The Jeep? The theft?*

Who on earth would believe me?

As they approached the ravine, the surrounding sounds began to fade. Kirsten felt as if her ears were clogged. She swallowed, but it didn't help.

Then she heard a low, familiar noise.

A moan.

"Virgil! Do you hear that?"

To her amazement, Virgil was leaning forward in his seat, eyes buggy. "Yes!"

"Ohhhhhhh!" It grew louder and louder until, just as they were passing the concrete guardrail, it made the Jeep vibrate like an echo chamber.

Kirsten skidded to a stop.

Virgil's hands were over his ears. He looked at Kirsten in disbelief. "Are you nuts? Go!"

"Virgil!" Kirsten was shouting. "Get out! You have to show me exactly where the crash site was!"

"What? No way!"

Kirsten got out of the Jeep, ran to Virgil's side, pulled open the door, and yanked him out.

"Stop!" Virgil protested.

But Kirsten did not let go. She pushed Virgil in front of her and yelled, "Show me! I have the keys, and we're not leaving!"

His hands still over his ears, Virgil looked into the ravine. "Okay. I know where there's a flashlight — or does Nguyen provide lighting?"

Without waiting for an answer, he went around to the back of the Jeep. He lifted the door and pulled out a thick flashlight with a handle. "Follow me!"

"GRRRRRUUUMMMB OHHHHSHAAA!"

The moaning was unbearable, words struggling to escape a mangled mouth. But Nguyen was nowhere to be seen.

Virgil kept the flashlight trained on the ground. Slowly he led Kirsten down the pathless embankment. She held on to branches and slender shoots, her shoes slipping on the leaves.

They seemed to be traveling aimlessly. Every few moments Virgil stopped, swinging the light beam around, trying to get his bearings. The moaning seemed to have taken physical form, replacing the oxygen around them. Kirsten found it hard to breathe.

Then, finally, when she could take it no longer, Virgil stopped. "There!" he shouted. "By that tree!"

In the path of the flashlight beam was a thick oak tree. About two feet off the ground, its trunk had been ripped open. A rough oval of smooth, blond wood gaped from within, surrounded by jagged fingers of split bark.

Here we are, Kirsten thought.

This was where Nguyen had left the world. And where his aunt and uncle had returned to sprinkle his ashes. Nguyen's body was here among the leaves and pine needles.

Virgil's lips were moving, but Kirsten couldn't hear him. Nguyen's voice seemed to be bending the trees, making the leaves turn away in fright.

She reached into her pocket and pulled out the chain. She held the locket in her right hand.

Then, digging her finger into a small ridge in its side, she sprang it open.

In the tiny space inside was a yellowing, faded photograph.

Two young faces, male and female, looked

obliquely at each other. The woman was wearing a gorgeous brocaded collar. Her mouth was grim and patient, her chin weak and almost indistinguishable from her neck. But Kirsten could not stop looking at her. Her eyes were like two small, dark jewels. Though tiny and faded and ancient, the photo had still not extinguished their fierce, fiery love.

This was what Nguyen wanted. What he longed for his whole life. What had been ripped away from him when he was too young to fight back. What he had given to a girl who hadn't loved him. His mother and father.

Kirsten looked upward, hoping now to see the hideous form their son had become.

Kirsten's hair blew across her face. She felt a sudden chill. Then a drop on her nose. Another on her cheek.

Around her, branches began to groan and bend in a sudden gale wind.

Thunder boomed nearby, barely audible through the moaning. Rain began to fall heavier.

"Oh, *no*!" Virgil shouted.

Or maybe it was "Let's go!" Kirsten couldn't tell. And she didn't care.

Virgil's flashlight was migrating all over the

place, but Kirsten could see the oak tree clearly. It was lit as Nguyen had been, from within, like a dream.

On the forest floor, in the growing gusts, leaves began to rustle. From among them, a thin grayish-black cloud swirled upward like the dust from a city sidewalk in a summer windstorm.

Kirsten felt herself being sucked toward the swirling gale. She tried to hold her ground, but it was impossible.

Virgil was shrieking at her now. *"GIVE IT TO HIM!"* she thought she heard him say.

The locket. Of course. She held it upward.

A hand landed on her shoulder. Hard.

Kirsten looked around.

Crrrackk!

A flash of lightning bathed the embankment in harsh green-whiteness. Directly above them a police car was parked along the road.

And a blue-uniformed man with a tense face was now pulling Kirsten toward it.

Chapter 28

"Don't!" Virgil shouted, grabbing her other arm. "Leave her!"

He lunged at the policeman, shining the flashlight in his face, pushing him backward.

The policeman let go. A partner, approaching behind him, grabbed Virgil in a hammer hold.

"GIVE HIM THE LOCKET, KIRSTEN!" Virgil bellowed.

His flashlight was swinging wildly. Kirsten caught a glimpse of the first policeman, scrambling to his feet.

She stepped closer to the tree, again lifting the locket high.

Before her, the dust was rising, whirlpooling furiously, thickening into a vague gray-black shape.

The policeman, gritting his teeth angrily,

stepped into the unearthly glow before her.

Before he could grab her, his feet left the ground. He rose upward like a leaf on a gentle breeze, his face locked in a mask of terror.

Then, as if flicked by a gigantic finger, he hurtled away and landed on the slope of the embankment.

In Kirsten's hand, the locket began to glow dull green.

The dust, thick and almost solid black, still in a frenzy of movement, was recognizable now. It had taken a human form — head, torso, arms, legs — all composed of swirling ashes.

Then the form began to move. Slowly its arm rose to mirror Kirsten's.

The locket's glow grew intense. Kirsten had to squint to avoid being blinded.

The moaning was changing now, becoming an explosive sob, a cry of joy.

BOOOOOOM!

The crack of thunder sent Kirsten flying. A flash of light obliterated everything around her, and she fell to the ground.

Pain shot up the right side of her body like an electric jolt.

When she opened her eyes, she was next to Virgil.

Behind him, two burly Port Lincoln cops were gaping, rubber-faced.

The moaning had stopped. The silence was so powerful, it made Kirsten nauseous.

"What happened?" Virgil's voice was muffled and tinny, with a high-pitched, metallic ring.

Kirsten grabbed his flashlight. She trained it on the ground before her. The dust was gone, the leaves resting as if they'd never been disturbed.

The light beam caught a tiny glint of metal near the base of the tree, and Kirsten went to it.

She pulled the chain out of a tangle of leaves and broken twigs. The locket was hanging open.

The photo was gone.

Kirsten smiled.

For the trumpet shall sound, she thought. *And death is swallowed up in victory.*

At last.

Screeeeee!

The sound of squealing tires made Kirsten look up. She quickly shone the flashlight toward the road.

The Jeep was tearing away. The light beam caught the unmistakable silhouette of Mr. Busk in the driver's seat.

"Get him!" Kirsten yelled to the cops.

She pointed the flashlight at them, from one to the other. Neither looked as if he'd heard her. Neither looked as if he were capable of moving. Or speaking.

With their eyes wide and glazed, their mouths slack, and their arms dangling uselessly, they reminded Kirsten of newborn babies.

She looked at Virgil. He looked at her.

Together they burst out laughing.

Epilogue

". . . So I didn't know why he wanted the locket, but I knew he did," Kirsten explained to the policeman, Officer Clark, as he drove slowly along Riverside Road.

"And, as you saw, she was right," Virgil added from the backseat. He nodded with a self-satisfied smile to the cop sitting next to him, who had finally managed to force his mouth closed.

"Anyway, that was why I broke the pawn-shop window," Kirsten continued. "Of course I wouldn't have done it if they'd been open."

"Of course," Officer Clark said with a wan nod. "Uh, any of you want a cup of coffee?"

Kirsten knew none of her explanation had registered. Which, to be honest, was just fine with her.

She shot Virgil a glance. He was trying hard

not to giggle. She wondered if he was thinking what she was: how to tell all of this to Maria.

"Hey," the other cop called out suddenly, "slow down!"

Officer Clark turned on his flashing lights. Kirsten squinted and saw the outline of a Jeep along the opposite side of the road, just before a sharp bend to the left.

"Uh-oh," Virgil said.

Officer Clark stopped by the side of the road, leaving on the flashers.

All four of them left the police car. Both Kirsten and Officer Clark aimed their flashlights at the Jeep as they approached.

Kirsten and Virgil looked inside. Mr. Busk was not there.

The two policemen searched around the Jeep, looking in the woods.

"Guess he ran out of gas," Virgil surmised.

"I'm not so sure," Kirsten said. She pointed her flashlight at the envelope full of flyers in the backseat.

The envelope was black around the edges. And open.

Kirsten swung the light around, onto the road. A few yards away lay a crumpled, charred, glossy piece of paper, facedown.

Just beyond it, slicing through a slick pattern

of leaves, were two solid, black tire tracks that curved around the bend in the road ahead.

"I can't look," Kirsten said.

Officer Clark came jogging onto the road, the paraphernalia on his belt jangling. He lit the tire tracks with his own flashlight.

Kirsten and Virgil watched silently as he ran to the bend and looked around. The beam of his flashlight disappeared down the unseen section of Riverside Drive.

Even in the flat light of Kirsten's beam, she could see Officer Clark blanch. He removed a two-way radio from his belt and held it to his mouth.

"Yeah, this is Clark, requesting an ambulance. Now."

As he gave the location, Kirsten picked up the flyer. She did not bother to read the contest rules for the best driver in Port Lincoln.

"Oh my God . . ." Virgil murmured.

They both stared at the middle of the page. At the gaping, empty space.

About the Author

Peter Lerangis is the author of another bizarre thriller, *The Yearbook*, as well as many movie novelizations under the pseudonym, A. L. Singer. Peter got his driver's license while he was a high-school senior in Freeport, New York, leaving no known casualties. Nowadays he drives a faded but glorious 1979 Chevrolet Impala, which he parks on the streets of New York City. He is hoping to win a newer car in a sweepstakes.

THRILLERS

Nobody Scares 'Em Like R.L. Stine

THRILLERS

D.E. Athkins
- ❏ MC45246-0 Mirror, Mirror $3.25
- ❏ MC45349-1 The Ripper $3.25
- ❏ MC44941-9 Sister Dearest $2.95

A. Bates
- ❏ MC45829-9 The Dead Game $3.25
- ❏ MC43291-5 Final Exam $3.25
- ❏ MC44582-0 Mother's Helper $3.50
- ❏ MC44238-4 Party Line $3.25

Caroline B. Cooney
- ❏ MC44316-X The Cheerleader $3.25
- ❏ MC41641-3 The Fire $3.25
- ❏ MC43806-9 The Fog $3.25
- ❏ MC45681-4 Freeze Tag $3.25
- ❏ MC45402-1 The Perfume $3.25
- ❏ MC44884-6 The Return of the Vampire $2.95
- ❏ MC41640-5 The Snow $3.25
- ❏ MC45680-6 The Stranger $3.50
- ❏ MC45682-2 The Vampire's Promise $3.50

Richie Tankersley Cusick
- ❏ MC43115-3 April Fools $3.25
- ❏ MC43203-6 The Lifeguard $3.25
- ❏ MC43114-5 Teacher's Pet $3.25
- ❏ MC44235-X Trick or Treat $3.25

Carol Ellis
- ❏ MC46411-6 Camp Fear $3.25
- ❏ MC44768-8 My Secret Admirer $3.25
- ❏ MC47101-5 Silent Witness $3.25
- ❏ MC46044-7 The Stepdaughter $3.25
- ❏ MC44916-8 The Window $2.95

Lael Littke
- ❏ MC44237-6 Prom Dress $3.25

Jane McFann
- ❏ MC46690-9 Be Mine $3.25

Christopher Pike
- ❏ MC43014-9 Slumber Party $3.50
- ❏ MC44256-2 Weekend $3.50

Edited by T. Pines
- ❏ MC45256-8 Thirteen $3.50

Sinclair Smith
- ❏ MC45063-8 The Waitress $2.95

Barbara Steiner
- ❏ MC46425-6 The Phantom $3.50

Robert Westall
- ❏ MC41693-6 Ghost Abbey $3.25
- ❏ MC43761-5 The Promise $3.25
- ❏ MC45176-6 Yaxley's Cat $3.25

Available wherever you buy books, or use this order form.

Scholastic Inc., P.O. Box 7502, 2931 East McCarty Street, Jefferson City, MO 65102

Please send me the books I have checked above. I am enclosing $_____ (please add $2.00 to cover shipping and handling). Send check or money order — no cash or C.O.D.s please.

Name _____ Age _____

Address_____

City_____ State/Zip_____
Please allow four to six weeks for delivery. Offer good in the U.S. only. Sorry, mail orders are not available to residents of Canada. Prices subject to change.

T294